# The Elder 13

*Robert MacNeill*

ISBN: 0692355774
ISBN-13: 978-0692355770

## DEDICATION

I dedicate this to my mother, Shirley; who never told me to not chase whimsy. Who read through the novel in its many infant stages and always reminded me "why not" instead of "why".

# ACKNOWLEDGMENTS

Once more I would like to acknowledge my mother for all she has done for me. My sister, Heather, who provided me with a sounding board when I needed it. My father, Bob, who honestly told me he would not enjoy read it. My fellow English teachers, football coaches, and educators for forcing me to never fit inside anyone's box.

# FROM SECTOR ONE GRAND WIRELESS SERVICE:

Another wonderful day in Sector One, from the Grand Ministers, no one should be concerned with the recent rumor of issues with Sector Two and Sector Five. There is no uprising, and our Grand Ruler has assured that nothing is out of the ordinary. Everyone from all Sectors must continue doing their part to improve life in our splendid land of perfection, and any thought of uprising will be met with swift re-education. Have a wonderful day, and remember we are watching everything.

# FROM LUKE'S DIARY:

A few days ago I was modified, and now my life is ruined. I am not sure if I will ever know how I will cope with this.

# PROLOGUE

## EDWARD

It began as such a nice day, when Edward woke from his deep sleep in his luxurious accommodations. Oak and marble covered the walls and surfaces, lighting bright enough to not require a squint, but soft enough to not cause a glare. The view screens that circled the main room are labeled Sector One all the way to Sector Seven. Each screen has multiple camera feeds, along with a plethora of data about the Sector the screen was monitoring.

Edward enjoyed watching Sector One as this was where the majority of the population lived, and he had the exclusive feed to any personal moment anyone in the Sector may have. Sitting down on his lounger, Edward decided to view a set of 11th form students having an illegal and unauthorized sexual encounter. He knew he should report the multiple infractions, but he was just going to enjoy the show, until the screen turned red and the building started to shake.

Edward quickly dressed and went upstairs to the meeting room on the top floor of the Elder Building. The commotion would soon cause panic in the Sector, but the other Elder 13 would have to solve this crisis.

Edward exited the lift and was greeted by five of the other Elder 13s. Stephanie and Richard were sitting on the extended lounger watching the screen showing Sector Two and Sector Five mobilizing for a fight. Michael and Susan were fixing drinks for the six of the Elder 13s who would eventually be on the floor. Finally Marcus was staring at the defense screen with such intensity that he was oblivious that Edward even showed up.

An explosion in the background shook the building as six of the Elder 13 sat around to decide what is next, as the war that will never end, raged around them. "Sector Two and Five are revolting" Stephanie remarked to her fellow members as Richard continued to stroke Stephanie's hair. Edward was always envious of these two's relationship, and while he has never be able to watch these two have any type of encounter, Edward just knew in his heart.

"Let them revolt, we can just destroy those two Sectors as well, use them for resources like Sector Three." Richard said, with an evil smile on his face. The face that always indicated that something extreme was about to happen. Michael and Susan brought the drinks to Richard and Stephanie and causing Stephanie to sit up to drink. Marcus drank his in one large gulp and Edward just stood holding the glass as a piece of the paint from the ceiling fell into his glass.

Outside, the missiles and bombs shook the buildings, reminding all of the legend of "The Blitz from Germany." The lights from the weapons light the night sky as if it was midday. Richard walked calmly to the other side of the room and pressed a button on the center screen of the room. Everything stopped. The sky turned dark, the world stood still, and The Elder 13 all knew that these two Sectors would never be a problem again.

Edward looked over at Richard and said, "That was a bit extreme wasn't it?"

Striding back to the lounger, Richard replied with no emotion in his voice, "I was tired of the racket."

"These two areas will allow us to increase our overall resources, and the decrease of those using those resources, is an all-around positive in my book." Susan remarked with a glance to the others as she entered her lift door to descend back to her residence.

# FROM THE LOST TEXTS OF THE GRAND AUTHORS (AS ALWAYS THIS IS BELIEVED TO NOT BE THE ORIGINAL VERSION OF THE TEXT):

The question is: is it better to be alive or dead? Is it nobler to put up with all the nasty things that luck throws your way, or to fight against all those troubles by simply putting an end to them once and for all? Dying, sleeping that's all dying is a sleep that ends all the heartache and shocks that life on earth gives us that's an achievement to wish for. To die, to sleep to sleep, maybe to dream. Ah, but there's the catch: in deaths sleep who knows what kind of dreams might come, after we've put the noise and commotion of life behind us. That's the consideration that makes us stretch out our sufferings so long. Who would choose to grunt and sweat through an exhausting life, unless they were afraid of something dreadful after death, the undiscovered country from which no visitor returns, which we wonder about without getting any answers from and which makes us stick to the evils we know rather than rush off to seek the ones we don't?

# SAMUEL

*Today is the day it all changes, I move on to the next chapter of my life.* Samuel stands in his apartment, looking at Beth, his wife, both knowing that this is the last time they will see each other for at least thirty years.

"Do you feel it?" Beth asked aloud.

"Looking in the glass. No of course not, I have not aged a day. But I am not sure where the last few decades have gone." Samuel responded, looking at his own young face in the glass.

"Will I see you in thirty years?" Beth asked to bring Samuel out of his own trance.

"Of course, I'll be waiting to greet you."

With this brief exchange, Samuel and Beth kissed goodbye and they both went to work. Samuel has spent the last year training his replacement as the Head of Sustenance. Jacob has picked up the job pretty easily; he spent the last 40 years over the shipping from Sector Five, the largest area. *I am sure he will be happy to move back to Sector One so he can see his wife every night.*

The tunnel ride felt shorter than usual, maybe because Samuel rode within the executive car for the first and last time. This car was the height of excess, the plastic benches were replaced by long leather couches, and a valet took your order and brought you a drink. Massage tables were set up to deliver the newest form of hydrocarbon electro-massage. This was the highlight of a lifelong lived, but Samuel started to feel uneasy, but the valet just brought him a nice cold carafe of pumpkin ale.

After a full revolution, Samuel and the others in the executive car egressed from the tunnel car and were driven to the Hall of the Future, where the five from the car will find out what the future holds for them. Five A.S.P.S. were waiting just outside the executive car, each with a different person's name in lights on the side. Samuel entered the one designated for him and the A.S.P.S. started to move.

The voice in the car reminded Samuel of a woman with a breathy voice; but also reminded him of an actual voice from his past. "Welcome Samuel, to the Automatic Speeding Propulsion System. I am happy to bring you to your destination of Hall of the Future, today. If there is anything you need from me, just go ahead and ask."

As usual when the A.S.P.S. said his name and destination, the voice paused for some reason. The voice brought Samuel back many years ago, right after his modification during his twenty-fifth year, when he was told he would be working in the newly developed Sector Two. The woman doing his procedure sounded exactly like this voice, but that was far too long ago for her to still be living; however the thought of that woman from all those years ago brought back a carnal desire from so long ago, a desire that was once satisfied by Beth, but for the next few decades wouldn't be satisfied.

The smooth ride took only a short time, but Samuel has started to notice that time passage seemed to speed up for him in many points. The cycle of seasons seem to take less and less time each year. "I guess this means that it will feel like only one or two years until I see Beth again, not thirty."

The A.S.P.S. recognizing the speech, but not understanding what it was supposed to do inquired, "I'm sorry Samuel, what is it you would like for me to do for you?" Again with the pause before his name.

Samuel knew what he wanted the original owner of this voice to do for him, but he could never bring himself to ask the machine to those types of things, Samuel meekly said, "Nothing" and closed his eyes. The ride continued as the images of this woman long forgotten flashed through his head; this woman replaced Beth in Samuel's memories for this one time.

A sudden jerk, brought Samuel out of his day dreams, as the A.S.P.S. came to a stop, the voice said, "Samuel, you have arrived at your destination of Hall of the Future. I hope you have a productive day." With this, the door opened and Samuel egressed and found himself at the front of the giant building of white marble, with large golden letters designating this building as the Hall of the Future. The large glass doors in the front are reflecting back on the outside, this is the only building with this trait; the only building Samuel has never been able to look into to see what was behind the walls.

Entering the doors, for the first time, Samuel was greeted by a vast area of nothingness. There was nothing behind the door except for a marble desk with no one sitting at it. Samuel found himself standing with a growing number of people for almost a half revolution, until a single man in a black pants, white shirt, and the most unusual black jacket. This jacket did not button all the up to the top, but left the majority of this man's front exposed to the elements; with only two buttons towards the bottom, only a single button near his stomach was being used, allowing the bottom to open freely. Around the man's neck was a black cloth, with an upside down triangle knot at the top of the shirt, with the remainder of the cloth covering the middle of the white shirt until the buttoned area of the jacket.

The man looked very strange to Samuel, and hopefully to the rest of the assembled group in this building. The man stopped at the edge of the marble desk, about fifteen paces from the front of the group, spoke, and "Welcome everyone to the Hall of the Future. Today, with respect to your long service to society, we have rewarded each of you with a relaxing retreat to Sector Seven. Once each of you are reunited with your family, you may choose to leave Sector Seven to enjoy the remainder of your days." A large smile filled this oddly dressed man, leaving Samuel feeling very relaxed. This is what many of his peers have been working so hard for all their working lives, with the hope to spend their non-working years in the bliss of Sector Seven.

Chairs appeared from under the floor, one for each of the society members in the lobby this morning. "Have a seat and someone will be along to gather each of you in their turn, and prepare you for your destination." Finishing this sentence, the man walked back down the hallway from where he came from and the future Sector Seven inhabitants sat and waited for their guide. Samuel was not called first which he was happy about, because he would have missed what happened once a person was called. The chair which the person was sitting in, once called and the person vacated it, would lower back in the floor. Eventually after about fifteen names, Samuel was called by the strangely dressed man from the original introduction.

Samuel did not get to see if his chair disappeared, as he was quickly brought down the corridor and into a room, where the man unbuttoned the single button on his jacket, and sat in his chair in front of his terminal. Samuel sat in the other chair, and the man began speaking, "Good morning, Samuel; I am Richard, and I will be helping you get ready to move to Sector Seven." Richard smiled, and this may have been the most unsettling smile Samuel had ever seen. "Now you have spent the last sixty years as the Head of Sustenance, is this correct?"

Samuel forgot how long he had actually been at that job, but he was correct, so Samuel simply dipped his head in acknowledgement. "Great," Richard continued, "and this is your two hundred and seventeenth name day?" Again, Samuel dipped his head. "Perfect, you have indicated that you would like to stay in Sector Seven for at the minimum of thirty years, to allow your wife to also reach the designated age, is this still correct?" Another dip and Richard continued to speak, "And what if Beth does not make the next thirty years? Would you like to continue to live in Sector Seven or would you like the option to be notified and reassess the situation at that point?"

Samuel had not thought about this eventuality. Sure, Beth would not age and pass away from anything so simple, but people still ended their lives early by various means, sometimes by their own hands. "I would like to be notified and be given the option to reassess."

"Perfect, is there anything you would like to do on the day you arrive?" At this question, a screen appeared in front of Samuel displaying all the options for what he could do once arriving in Sector Seven. The list had so many great options like: underwater tours, riding various animals, and various extreme activities like free falling from the sky with something called a chute. After scanning the list Samuel indicated he would like to go to something called a BBQ. Richard nodded his head, "That is an amazing culinary experience you shall never forget. You read to depart for Sector Seven?" Another dip from Samuel, and the two of them rose from their chairs, and Richard buttoned his single button again, and opened the door for Samuel to leave the room before him.

The two walked down the corridor towards the door marked Sector Seven, when they arrived, Richard put his hand on Samuel's shoulder, a gesture Samuel was not familiar with and Samuel walked through the doorway. On the other side was just another room, only this one was totally black, like Richard's suit, but there was nowhere to sit. After a few moments, Samuel heard a noise and felt his whole body give way to gravity as he felt himself plummet into the darkness. A giant fire was waiting for Samuel at the bottom of the drop where he laid with broken legs and was burned alive, until Samuel passed out from the sensation.

# FROM SECTOR ONE GRAND WIRELESS SERVICE:

Recently, a new Grand Ruler has been named since Johnny Whiteneck had stepped down from a record high approval rating. The Sectors are doing better than ever, and there has not been a major issue for as long as this reporter has been journaling. Going back into records, you would have a hard time to find anything since the Sector Five strike, which only lasted a few standard units.

# MICHAEL

"I am getting tired" Michael said as he walked into the top floor of the Hall of the Future, where screens lined the walls labeled Sector One through Sector Seven.

"Then go back to sleep," Richard said without looking back towards Michael staring at the screen marked Sector Seven, where a replay of the yesterday's retreats was taking his undivided attention. Laughter broke out when one of the women fell into a large tank of water, and the top lowered, forcing her to breath the water until she expired. Michael looked away in disgust, he never enjoyed watching the expiration, but Richard just loves to re-watch them.

"That's not what I am saying and you know it." Michael responded with defeat in his voice. Standing on the top floor in his normal attire of a green floor length coat and shorts. His shirts were his pride of his wardrobe, as he had many promoting classical music. The one today was for a band named "Pink Floyd" a band from several thousand years ago, but he never tires of them. His short pants ended blow his knees and had what Michael called "Frays" at the bottom.

"What's wrong babe?" Susan asked leaning on the center counter which separates the lounging area with the monitors and the sustenance area with the drinks and food. As usual she looked stunning, wearing a long silk dress, what used to be called an evening gown. Michael could not help his eyes but follow the v shape front of the dress which seemed to never end and come to its point, until right above her navel. Today's dress was a dark forest green, and the dip in the front was only exceeded by the cut up the side, which stopped right at the start of her hip. Michael never could get over the absolute beauty of her, and wished to two of them could spend the night of unauthorized sexual encounter, but this was prohibited by The Laws of the Elder 13.

After a long pause, Susan performed her normal routine of showing Michael a small portion of the body he lusted after. She pulled the opening of her dress to the side to allow one of her breast to fall free; her milky weight skin was only interrupted by the perfect pink circles of her nipple. Once Michael got his eye full, she pulled her dress back in place and said, "Okay, so now will you speak?"

Michael shook his hair, allowing his long brown hair to shake wildly, which once out of place and wild looking, he pulled the fronts behind his ears to once again look normal. "Sorry, but…"

"…But you want to bend me over and have an unauthorized sexual encounter with me. I know." Susan finished.

"No, well, yes. But what I was going to say was…never mind. I am getting tired of all of this." This caught the attention of the rest of the Elder 13 who was upstairs and they all gathered around. "I am tired of daily expirations. I am tired that we are not actually part of the society we govern. I am tired of being so powerful. But mainly, I am tired of still being alive." This last statement, was said at a very loudly as if Michael had been waiting to say this for years and it finally boiled out of the top of him. The statement forced a few of the Elder 13 to laugh, led by Richard, until they saw the straight face of Michael and stopped.

"Why would you be tired of this?" Richard responded as he motioned around the room with his arms. "We live past the two hundred and seventeenth year mark, and we never age. We can do anything we want, and only we can stop each other. Besides, stop whining, you have only just passed your five hundred and fifty-third name day. You are young even by our standards."

This was true, Michael, while not the youngest of the Elder 13, that honor belonged to Frederick with only two hundred and seventy-three years, was young. Frederick was chosen after a fifteen year vacancy in the Elder 13, after Max died suddenly when he fell into the Sector Seven BBQ retreat and was burned alive with the intended expiree. Frederick wore the normal fashion of the time, the jumpsuit, except instead of the normal colors of grey, black, green, and red; he chooses to wear blue with the grey, black, green, and red as accent colors on the edges instead of the traditional blue. Frederick is the least fashionable of the Elder 13, but he refuses to change the attire he is used to wearing.

Michael just looked at his fellow Elder 13s, and began to walk out of the room, when Edward came from one of the rooms lining the corridor and said, "What exactly is the issue with still being alive?"

Michael just stared at Edward, who until now was supposed to be out of the sector, and sighed. "I remember when I was originally selected to part of the Elder 13, I found it to be a huge honor, but I have been doing it for over three hundred years, it seems that the days go by too quickly, the years are passing faster, and my memory is the only part of me which ages. Every day I look in the damn looking glass and see the same face I have seen for five hundred years, and not a George damned thing changes. Everyone I knew in my before life has now been retired, and many of them I have watched personally expire. But now I just want to go into the nothingness everyone else is promised in Sector Seven." This plea from Michael seemed to take all of his energy out of his soul, and Susan helped him back to the couch.

"Of course you are getting tired, but we serve the ultimate purpose. We keep everything working and I hope you have figured it out by now, Sector Seven does not exist." Marcus Said sitting down beside Michael. "If we retire, if we expire, then the Elder 13 will have to train another before it is ready, and the votes could become even and tie. You remember what that was like, but there is a way for all to become right, if you really want to go down this path, and George knows it is a decision which you cannot turn back from."

## FROM THE LOST TEXTS OF THE GRAND AUTHORS (AS ALWAYS THIS IS BELIEVED TO NOT BE THE ORIGINAL VERSION OF THE TEXT):

The whole world is a stage, and all the men and women merely actors. They have their exits and their entrances, and in his lifetime a man will play many parts, his life separated into seven acts. The infant, schoolboy, lover, soldier, judge, skinny man, and second childhood: without teeth, without eyes, without taste, without everything.

# RICHARD

Traveling down to the lobby of the Hall of the Future from where Richard was just listening to Michael rant on about how he was getting tired of this life, was making Richard feel anger towards his fellow Elder 13. We know what we agreed to when we agreed, so why is he whinging about it now?

It was Richard's turn to do the introduction to the new retirees and he could not be any happier about this than if he was also allowed to personally retire all of these puppets himself, with his own two hands. Richard reached the ground floor of the Hall of the Future and looked at himself in the large looking glass. He was perfect looking, his tie has a perfect knot, his shoes were a perfect shiny black, and there was not a hair out of place, and not a wrinkle in his black suit. Today he decided to go with a bone-white shirt, instead of the off-white, pearl-white or white-white shirt. He loved the way his shoes sounded as he walked down the hall; he thought this must be what the old kings drums used to sound like, because he was the king.

He arrives to see the newest group of retirees and said, "Welcome everyone to the Hall of the Future. Today, with respect to your long service to society, we have rewarded each of you with a relaxing retreat to Sector Seven. Once each of you are reunited with your family, you may choose to leave Sector Seven to enjoy the remainder of your days." Richard could feel his large smile fill his face as he always did during this part of the speech. Richard continued with, "Have a seat and someone will be along to gather each of you in their turn, and prepare you for your destination." Once he stopped he walked back down the hallway knowing at this point the chairs would appear and everyone would sit down.

"I love this part," Richard said as he entered the chamber where the other Elder 13 were waiting on him. He was the only one that enjoyed the opening speech that they did every morning, but he mostly loved watching the separate retirements. Recently, Alice came up with some new first day activities for the retirees to pick from, which currently will be ready next week. One is called a "Shish Kabob" something from before the massacre where people would take meats and pierce it with metal or wood and then it would be enjoyed by someone. Richard came up with using this idea, to help the people expire.

"How many today?" Alice said coming towards Richard in her denim leggings, which did not extend very far down her legs. She called them "Cut-offs" another fashion from the mid to late 20th century along with a button-up shirt that only a few buttons where buttoned, allowing the bottom to be tied in a not, not like the elegant knot Richard has daily on his tie but a knot Richard uses for his shoes, and the top to allow the top portions of her tan breast to be visible and pushed up as if they were trying to escape the whole outfit. Richard despised the way she dressed, at least Susan dresses elegantly, but Alice shows no class in the way she dresses, probably because she did not come from the higher society in Sector One.

"26 for the first shift, then the second group will come at midday and another 31 will be with that group." As the two shifts broke up, Richard, who always was on the first group headed towards his office to look into the first retiree he would be dealing with. Maxwell, a sustenance gatherer from Sector Two. Because of this, Richard knew he would need a thorough cleansing once he was done with this gatherer.

Richard rose from this desk to walk back to the waiting area, where he realized that several of the Elder 13 had already gotten their first pick of the day. "Maxwell, will you follow me?" As he finished the sentence, Richard turned around and started walking back towards his office. After the two sat down, Richard started his normal routine, "Good morning, Maxwell; I am Richard, and I will be helping you get ready to move to Sector Seven." Smile and continue, "Now you have spent the last one hundred and sixty years as a sustenance gatherer in Sector Two, is this correct?" Richard knew it was correct, but he had to wait for this slime to answer to the affirmative. Why did he never try to move up in the rankings? Why was he happy just to do this job for the last one hundred and sixty years? Why in George's great name would someone do this? Maxwell finally tilted his head that he was correct.

"Perfect," Richard continued, "and this is your two hundred and seventeenth name day?" Again another wait while this simpleton decided if today he was two hundred and seventeen or not, when if he was not, then there would be no use of him being here in the Hall of the Future. Another dip. "Great, you have indicated that you would like to stay in Sector Seven for at the minimum of two years, as your wife arrived thirteen years ago and she wanted to stay for fifteen total, is this still correct?" Another dip allowing Richard to continued, " I am not sure if you knew this, but your wife is waiting to meet you upon arriving at Sector Seven, and has said she is looking forward to seeing you and spending the next two years falling back in love with you. Another smile, another dip.

"Great, now there is one last thing, before you meet up with your wife, is there anything you would like to do on the day you arrive?" The screen appeared in front of Maxwell, displaying all the options for what he could do once arriving in Sector Seven.

Maxwell stared at the list as if he had never been given a choice in his whole worthless life. Several minutes passed before Maxwell spoke. "There is so much to choose from, what would you pick?"

Richard hated this questions, he would never have to make the choice, and because he knows what it all means, it is like asking how you would like to expire. But as always he was prepared for this, and he picked one of his favorite to watch. "Many people say they enjoy going to the antique firearm exhibit. You will get to see many old killing devices and will get to experience the firing of several of them during the day. Also people enjoy mountain climbing. Lastly people really enjoy seeing the different types of animals."

Maxwell started to turn red, and spoke very softly, "I have always been a fan of the old spectros of people hiking along mountains; I think I would like to do that before I meet up with Heather."

Richard was a little disappointed, he was hoping for the animal or the firearm exhibit, but this will be fun to watch either way. Richard stood as he motioned towards the door; allowing Maxwell to follow him down the hall to one of the doors marked Sector Seven, and allowed Maxwell to enter. Richard did not hurry back to his office to watch the monitor to watch this worthless creature hang on to the side of a cliff. This was a battle of stamina, Maxwell had three choices, he could continue climbing up, and get to the top and freeze to expiration over the course of several hours, he could hang and climb until his arms gave out and fall to his expiration, or he could try to climb down, only to find a cave where a giant animal will come and tear his body apart until expiration. Richard disliked this one, because it sometimes took hours or even days for the expiration to happen.

Richard remembered three people at once being in this area and it lasting almost a week, because of body heat, and the last one ate the other two. While that part was very entertaining, it was not the quick ending he enjoyed so much. So Richard resolved himself to go and gather the next lucky person, maybe they will provide a more entertaining retirement for Richard to watch.

Richard began his walk back to the lobby of the Hall of the Future when he saw Alice in her Cut-offs shorts about to grab the next expired piece of meat. Her shorts seemed to be shorter than usual, or the more of her rounded bottom appeared beneath the edges of the shorts. As she walked towards her office, he saw that he breast were pressed more out of her shirt than normal and she was looking very tasty. Richard moved into an alcove in the hallway after Alice's office, hiding from her and started to instantly feel hatred for his feelings, as Alice was low born, and not up to the standard he places for his unauthorized sexual encounter. But if he were to do something about it, at least it would be in the lawless room.

## FROM THE LOST TEXTS OF THE GRAND AUTHORS (AS ALWAYS THIS IS BELIEVED TO NOT BE THE ORIGINAL VERSION OF THE TEXT):

Oh, poor Yorick! I used to know him a very funny guy, and with an excellent imagination. He carried me on his back a thousand times, and now, how terrible, this is him. It makes my stomach turn. I don't know how many times I kissed the lips that used to be right here. Where are your jokes now? Your pranks? Your songs? Your flashes of wit that used to set the whole table laughing? You don't make anybody smile now. Are you sad about that?

# ALICE

Alice loved the walk from the main lobby of the Hall of the Future back to her office, because it allowed for these retirees to watch the way a woman should walk from behind. She swayed her hips as her cheeks peaked from the bottom of her short shorts. Alice could feel the eyes of the remaining thirteen, two hundred and seventeen year olds all just staring at her back end, and relished in the feeling. Every eye moving with her every move, men adjusting themselves, women having strange feelings they had never thought of before.

Alice only enjoyed retiring the men each day because she would try and convince them to do one of her specially created first day arrival activities. The best part about these activities, Alice has created the room with cameras which remained off until she allows for them to be turned on. So the first half of each expiration has zero documentation, and that is the way Alice prefers it. Today she was being followed by Marc, a man of importance to Sector One; yesterday he was the head of Information Dissemination for all Sectors. As the two walk towards Alice's office, she could feel Marc's eyes fall on her backside, and a smile crossed her face. But up ahead, a man in a black suit looked to be spying on her.

*Richard, that self-centered wanker, is spying on me* Alice thought thinking of all the times Richard had blown her off and made her feel like trash just because of where she came from, but that was over six hundred years ago, before the rebellion, she was one of the Elder 13 during the eradication of her home in Sector Five. Alice had to put all this out of her mind as she turned into her office and focus all of her attention to Marc.

As they both sat down, Alice started the talk. "Good morning, Marc; I am Alice, and I will be helping you get ready to move to Sector Seven." Alice did not smile but just gave a sultry look towards Marc and continued, "Now you have spent the last thirty-seven years as the head of Information Dissemination for all Sectors, is that correct doll?" With the word doll, another look and a lick of her lips causing Marc to catch a lump in his throat and start to shift uncomfortably. Finally he dipped his head and Alice was free to continue, "And this is your two hundred and seventeenth name day?"

After each question, Alice would give a look, a wink or something to boil the blood of this man on his last day of his limited eternal life. Another dip. "Well now, you have indicated that you would like to stay in Sector Seven for at the minimum of ten years, as your husband expired before his time and does not get the pleasure of coming to Sector Seven. So what happened to your husband?"

"He was hit by an A.S.P.S. while he was

collecting people to come here about twenty-five years ago." Marc responded.

"And since then, you have been alone?" Alice asked, reaching across the surface to grasp his hands.

"I'm not sure 'alone' is the word I would use, but I did not remarry." Marc winked at Alice, the first sign of life which drove Alice to push the encounter even farther. "Now there is one last thing, before you start your life in Sector Seven, is there anything you would like to do on the day you arrive?" The screen appeared in front of Marc, displaying all the options for what he could do once arriving in Sector Seven.

As the screen slid in front of Marc, he spoke, "Excuse me Mum, I have been dealing with information all my life, since my modification at twenty-five, and I know nothing about Sector Seven. I receive updates from the Sector, but it always reports that everything is 'perfect', and that is just hard to believe."

Alice was a bit taken aback, she needed to let Edward know about this, he might need to change up the reports more to show a slight deviation so questions like this does not become common. Not showing any shock on her face, Alice simply giggled and whispered in Marc's ear, "You will understand soon enough" and sent her hand to caress his thigh. "So what is it you would like to do when you arrive?" Trying to get Marc back on the task of deciding how he shall expire.

After looking at the screen for a while, Marc asked, "Well there is a Sector which is labeled 'Alice's Recommendation,' what is that about?"

This was Alice's favorite questions, these were

the retreats that only Alice did, and she designed them all herself. "These are just some of my favorite ones that I recommend because I always receive positive feedback."

After reading the lists of titles Marc asked, "What is a Carnal Cannibal Cafe?"

"Ah, the Triple C. I have heard nothing but great things about that. It is a tasting menu of sorts, where you are the guest of honor. There is a small hint of an unauthorized sexual encounter, but it is just a great meal, and it will make your first day in Sector Seven one no one will forget." Alice said with a Cheshire grin.

The two left the office and arrived at one of the many doors marked for Sector Seven, and Marc opened and walked in. Upon crossing the threshold a needle stuck in his neck and he was instantly put to sleep. The arms came down and placed Marc on the waiting four post oak bed, and stripped him of his clothing. Several holos of naked men and women appeared around Alice, and another injection woke Marc right up. His eyes darted around taking in the scene, and he took in the sights. His manhood began to swell when Marc noticed Alice walking towards him slowly taking off her top. She climbed onto the bed and whispered in his ear, "Welcome to Sector Seven, I am going to start by taking you in my mouth."

Marc started to smile until a sharp pain nearly caused him to pass out. Alice slowly put Marc's full length in her mouth and quickly bit down to sever the appendage with one bite. The blood started to flow quickly from the severing and a small fire next to the bed rose up, and Alice spit the piece of flesh onto the fire. "I never enjoy it raw, just rare." Alice started to laugh, and took a knife and started to carve Marc's pectoral muscles out of his chest and placing them on the grill. Marc expired at one point during this butchering but Alice would not be satisfied until she had a few days' worth of food.

# FROM SECTOR ONE GRAND WIRELESS SERVICE:

Recently a group calling themselves "The Watched" have said that everything is actually run by a small group of immortals who dispatch anyone who disagrees with them, and they can be seen all around the community. A spokesman from "The Watched" who refused to give their name has stated that if anyone was to look closely, they would see these individuals, as they always dress differently from anyone else.

When reached for comment, The Grand Ruler said that there is no great immortal body over the government, and that these people are just trying to drive attention away from whatever they are doing wrong.

# LUKE

Turning off his monitor in his accommodations and just sat shaking his head. The pollution of the Elder 13 has been happening for some time. Luke could remember when it used to be much more pure; the members of the Elder 5 never had this problem. There was never issues of cannibalism, Elder's being sexual with each other, or anything which is plaguing the group now.

Luke did not attend many of the daily gatherings the Elder 13 have, but he always was watching. His part of the group was not only leadership and making the tough decisions, but he worked with the modification, not the retirement. Luke enjoyed the elongation of life, not the retirement of the immortality he provides.

Walking over to his closet he pulled out his robes, the same style he wore before it all changed, when he first was modified. He struggled to find the words some days to describe what each part was, but he never forgot the term "vestments." The garments were simple enough, it was a black shirt, buttoned to the top with a white collar which only showed in the front, a long black robe and sometimes he would wear red robes with a four corner hat, or some purple adornments on his vestments on what he called "Special Occasions."

On his walk towards the lift, and entered to go down to the underground, he did not need to go to the Hall of the Future, but few buildings over to the Modification Center. The walk under the streets was always peaceful as Luke started to recite his ancient rituals which involved moving beads through his fingers while repeating a long series of memorized passages.

"In the name of the Father, and of the Son and of the Holy Spirit. Amen. I believe in God, the Father Almighty, Creator of heaven and earth; and in Jesus Christ, His only Son, our Lord; Who was conceived by the Holy Spirit, born of the Virgin Mary, suffered under Pontius Pilate, was crucified, died, and was buried. He descended into hell; the third day He arose again from the dead. He ascended into heaven, and sits at the right hand of God, the Father Almighty; from thence He shall come to judge the living and the dead. I believe in the Holy Spirit, the Holy Catholic Church, the communion of Saints, the forgiveness of sins, the resurrection of the body and life everlasting. Amen." Luke was muttering under his breath.

Luke was annoyed that by the time he reached his destination he did not finish his full ritual, "Hail Mary, full of grace, the Lord is with thee; blessed art thou among women, and blessed is the fruit of thy womb, Jesus. Holy Mary, Mother of God, pray for us sinners, now and at the hour of our death. Ahh damn, I guess I will not finish today."

Luke arrived at the lift for the Modification Center and rose to the ground floor, where he would start the mass counseling of the group on their twenty-fifth name day, and preparing for their new semi-immortal life. Today's group was, like usual, a larger group than the retirement group each day, and with much more passion and energy. Walking into the room, a hush fell over the group as these members of society witnessed the first person dressed oddly in their short lives.

"Hello everyone, I am Luke, and I am going to be talking to you all about the modification you will all receive today. Before we begin, does anyone have any questions?" Luke asked, knowing the first question he would be ask, as it is the first question he had been asked nearly every day since taking this position.

"You look different, why is your face all wrinkled?" A tall blonde male said without thinking that this might in some way be offensive.

"You are very perceptive, I received the modification a few years later than my twenty-fifth name day, and thus I have retained the body and face I had at that time. This is why for the last five years, you have been told to eat right, get in shape, and try to stay healthy." Luke responded, much as he has for the last four hundred years of dealing with this specific job. Luke was one of the original recipients of the modification in its current form, as the government wanted to know if it would not just keep people alive, but would it actually make someone younger. It did not.

From the other side of the room a brown haired woman asked, "How many years did you wait?"

Another question Luke was very used to answer. "One. That is why we chose this name day, one year and you look like me." At this statement, Luke put his hands by his face to emphasize the aged lines of his face and began to laugh, which allowed for laughter to fill the room. The truth is that he was an additional twenty-five years from the standard twenty-five, making Luke the oldest person in both modified age, and actual years living, living within the sectors.

Luke began his favorite part of his day, the open question part of the day. The unmodified were always much more open and fun to be around, before the ravages of timeless time started the drain on a person's personality. "So what questions do you all have?"

"Is it true that this procedure will freeze us in time?" A short redheaded man asked from the side.

"Yes and no. It will freeze you in the sense that you will no longer age, thus you cannot expire from age, but just because you became very strong and buff, does not mean you will remain that way without still working out and eating right. You will need to do a minimal amount of exercise a day to maintain your current physique. We will let you know exactly what you will need to do." Luke answered again with a smile.

A small black haired woman in the middle asked, "Is it true we are done knacking?"

"Well, that is a very complicated questions. You are no longer allowed to have 'unauthorized sexual encounter' which is what we call 'knacking' once you are modified. As a fun note, before it is modified your sexual encounters were also illegal. Not that we cause trouble with unmodified for their illegal and unauthorized sexual encounters but once modified you will have to limit yourself to authorized sexual encounters only." Luke replied, but after a brief pause and a sea of blank faces, which all just looked confused, Luke added, "You have to get permission before having 'a bit of how's your father'."

Everyone laughed at this reference and began to nod. A tall muscular man asked a follow up questions, "Is it hard?"

Luke quickly responded, "Depends on how randy you are." Everyone laughed and once it all subsided Luke continued, "It is not difficult to get permission, but settling down with a single partner or set of partners, is the easiest way to maintain permission. Any questions not relating to authorized sexual encounters?"

From the back, a small meek voice spoke up, "Is it true we can't die after this?"

Luke hated this question the most. "Well, that is an interesting question. You can still die, just not naturally. You will not get sick, nor will your body start to break down and you will never succumb to age expiring you, but if you step in front of an A.S.P.S. or fall off a cliff, or something accidental, you can expire early."

"So, what is Sector Seven?" With this, Luke's head started to search, as he saw Laura, the only one of the Elder 13 he would to retire allow to lead the Elders. She was standing in the doorway, looking the same age as the rest of the members of society sitting in the room, but she was dressed in a pair of black leggings, which she called "yoga pants", which did nothing but make Luke stare at her bum and sweater from a former university from across the great ocean.

The name of the institution was always lost on Luke, but it was a series of two capital letter "T"'s stacked atop each other with a three dimensional effect with alternating red and black. She rotated the color of the sweater but never the logo. This was the university she was attending right before the great change, and she has been with Luke since they both received their own modification.

"Excuse me?" Luke said with a shake of his head. This was not a question usually asked. It was randomly asked once every few years, so the mystery of what happens after your two hundred and seventeenth name day remains an urban legend.

"I have heard that there is actually seven sectors, not just six. So is that true, or is that just a wild rumor." This question is never asked the same way twice, or if it is Luke never remembers how it was asked years before. So Luke paused, for a long time, composing the best way to answer the questions which would not be asked again for another year or another thirty years.

Slowly Luke responded, "Sector Seven is our retirement sector. Upon your two hundred and seventeenth name day, if nothing unfortunate has happened to you, you live out the rest of your life in retirement. You will be rewarded with being allowed to do almost any activity you have been wanting to do, and it is our government's way of saying 'Thank you' for all you have done between now and then."

After another long pause, where Luke allowed

everyone to take this information in, he franticly added, "But please do not go around telling people this, we like it to be a surprise." This would insure that everyone gathered would quickly spread this tale.

Standing up, Luke motioned towards Laura and the rest of the modifiers and said, "When you are called, please go with your attendant and you will receive your modification. My first for the day is Seymour." A shorter man stood up and followed Luke towards his modification room.

## FROM THE LOST TEXTS OF THE GRAND AUTHORS (AS ALWAYS THIS IS BELIEVED TO NOT BE THE ORIGINAL VERSION OF THE TEXT):

My mistress is in love with a monster. While she was sleeping in her bed of flowers, a group of bumbling idiots, rough workmen, got together. The stupidest one sat in the bushes. I took that opportunity to stick a donkey's head on him. Later, he came out of the bushes and everyone saw him. His friends ran away fast. They were all so afraid that they completely lost their common sense. They started to become scared of inanimate objects, terrified by the thorns and briars that catch at their clothing and pull off their sleeves and hats. I led them on in this frightened, distracted state, and left her there, transformed into someone with a donkey's head. At that exact moment, she woke up and immediately fell in love with him, a donkey.

# LAURA

Standing in her yoga pants and Texas Tech sweatshirt, she leaned against the wall listening to Luke go through his daily routine about the modification. Fifteen years ago, she set today to be the next day she would ask her question, so when she received her notification; she was filled with a giant sense of excitement because this always tripped Luke up. She loved watching him squirm under this question, because his former life comes out, and he has trouble with the lie. Waiting for her chance to ask her question, she started to think back when she was originally selected to be the part of the experimental phase of the program when she celebrated her twenty-third name day.

Laura had just graduated early from her university, and was given a chance to use her advanced degree in Environmental Toxicology in a lab in the United European Kingdoms. A year passed, and the world's environmental resources were not sustaining the influx of people coming from the outer regions, so her team was asked to create a cure for the toxicity of the plague of unwanted humans.

Laura and her team, after a year of research, proposed that such a cure would take almost one hundred years to fully disperse and for the complete ramification to be felt.

Laura's team was told to choose one person who could continue to work on the problem, and she was put forth, as the youngest, she had the greatest chance of seeing this through, but two days later she was brought to a lab with a Cardinal, a Medical Doctor, a Teacher, and an Engineer, where they were told they would undergo a procedure that would extend their life.

Laura came out of her daze when she heard Luke say, "You will not get sick, nor will your body start to break down and you will never succumb to age expiring you, but if you step in front of an A.S.P.S. or fall off a cliff, or something accidental, you can expire early."

George if this isn't the truth, Laura thought, then asked the question she had been waiting to ask all morning, "So, what is Sector Seven?"

"Excuse me?" Luke said with a shake of his head.

A smile was trying to emerge on Laura's face, but she kept it at bay. "I have heard that there is actually seven sectors, not just six. So is that true, or is that just a wild rumor."

Luke responded slower than usual. He hated this lie, but it was the necessary lie to keep the piece. So he began the lie he tells whenever he has to, "Sector Seven is our retirement sector. Upon your two hundred and seventeenth name day, if nothing unfortunate has happened to you, you live out the rest of your life in retirement. You will be rewarded with being allowed to do almost any activity you have been wanting to do, and it is our government's way of saying 'Thank you' for all you have done between now and then. But please do not go around telling people this, we like it to be a surprise."

The rest of the modifiers formed a line with Luke and Laura at either side, and each called their respective person's name. Laura's first modifier was a woman named "Layla." She was short with red hair and a beautiful smile, but he walk and thought something about her told Laura she was used to getting whatever she wants and if things did not go her way, there would be trouble. She was wearing the required grey jumpsuit and it fit her form nicely.

As the two walked into Laura's office, Laura instructed Layla, "Lie down on the table and make yourself comfortable. Before we begin do you have any questions about what is about to happen?" Laura was used to describing the procedure to the modifiers, which always puzzled her. When it happened to her, she was one of the first to go through the modification, but someone should have told these people what to expect. But it seems that everyone knows what to expect every day of their lives except on their twenty-fifth name day and their two hundred and seventeenth name day; these are always a surprise.

Layla began stalking very speaking very rapidly, asking the same questions most people ask, just with a hint of extra attitude, and the speed of a run-away A.S.P.S. "So, is it going to hurt? What will you do? How long will it take? What exactly are you going to do? What will you use? Have you cleaned all your items? What gives you the right to be doing this? Are you even trained? I have things to do so I need to know these things. Oh, and will this affect the rest of my day? Because if I understood that Luke guy out there, I have today to get all the necking I can get until I do some 'randy paperwork.' So are you going answer?" She finally stopped talking. Laura stared for a moment trying to take all the questions in, hoping not to miss one.

Laura just smiled and nodded as she listened to Layla rattle off her questions, and then spoke, slowly and methodically. Laura loved to do this to fast talkers, just speak slower than usual. "Well, were do I begin with those questions? I shall answer them all, so that completes the last question." Laura smiled, and Layla did not look amused. This was what Layla was not used to, not getting her way. Laura continued, "The modification will take one standard unit, while I have not cleaned the items, they have all been cleaned by a professional whose job it is to clean these materials. The government gives me the right to do this, as it is my profession, and I have been doing this job longer than you have been living." Laura paused at this and thought, I have been doing this longer than anyone alive has been alive except a ten of the Elder 13.

Continuing, "While you do have the rest of the day to have a 'bannger and mash party', you really should take it easy after the modification, and yes tomorrow you will be required to get authorization before engaging in any type of sexual activity. The amount of pain people report varies from person to person, but it is no more painful than your standard hydrodynamic gastro-intestinal cleansing or a simple electro epidermal follicular expelling; however, some have claimed no discomfort. Now what am I going to do exactly? That becomes quite technical, your body naturally creates a through a process called mitochondria creates oxidative phosphorylation, which forces your body to break itself down. What I will be doing today is removing the possibility of oxidative stress by using a synthetic serum which will prevent this from happening, and force your body to constantly create non-mutating replication of cells."

Laura stopped and looked at Layla's blank face, and then asked, "Any more questions before we begin?"

Robert MacNeill

# FROM SECTOR ONE GRAND
# WIRELESS SERVICE:

A message from the Hall of the Future was intercepted the other day, which The Grand Ruler and the workers in the Hall of the Future denied its authenticity. The message was only, "Don't Trust Us" over and over again. One worker from the Hall of the Future came forward and said that this was just a fun joke that people around the Hall play from time to time. Everyone has been instructed to go about their business and not to ask any more questions.

# KEVIN

Swinging his head from side to side, Kevin was entranced by the length of his hair. Several hundred years ago he found a relic of a time before modification where entertainment was not done through halos, but through a magnetized strip with a series of small still photos, when ran through a light source at a certain speed, showed an image on the wall, and this is where Kevin decided what his new look would be. His black hair was long, and straight, much like many of the women he dealt with the main difference that his slender figure did not make him look like any woman he ever met.

Along with the hair, Kevin always wore black pants made from modified cow carcass and a black shirt with a plunging neck, and no sleeves. He never wore any attire with sleeves, because he already had something Kevin always referred to as his "sleeves" and that was the series of inked markings on his arms that started at his clavicle, and rounded towards the back covering his scapula, lean arms, ending at the finish of his carpus. This was on both sides, filled with images of ancient markings resembling human remains, botanistic relics, and ancient references to the ancient literature of the time pre-modification.

Kevin was a very slender man, but he made up for it with his voice, a dark deep voice that should come from a much larger man, exuded from his lips. This voice would never put people at ease during his retirement interviews, but as he was to introduce the midday group, Kevin knew that around thirty persons would be coming to this midday group, which mostly where people who reside in the various other Sectors. These people were usually tougher men and women because they worked hard every day to insure the livelihood that all the rest of the United European Kingdom enjoyed.

As he walked towards the group sitting the lobby, he knew his hair was getting in his face as he walked, but Kevin had a saying, "Long hair, and don't care." The group where a mixture from all the difference Sectors, but it was obvious they wanted to make a good impression so they cleaned up very nice, wearing a clean jumpsuit for their trip to Sector One on the way to Sector Seven. Kevin stood in front of the group and said, "Welcome everyone to the Hall of the Future. Today, with respect to your long service to society, we have rewarded each of you with a relaxing retreat to Sector Seven. Once each of you are reunited with your family, you may choose to leave Sector Seven to enjoy the remainder of your days."

Kevin disliked this speech, but not for the same reason Edward and Michael did. Those two felt the Elder 13 were lying to the masses, but Kevin did not have a problem with this. He just felt it was a waste of time to pontificate for so long before having to get on with it. "Have a seat and someone will be along to gather each of you in their turn, and prepare you for your destination." Finishing his speech, Kevin turned knowing that his hair would cascade around his head as he moved his body, allowing himself the pleasure of pulling it out of his face.

Kevin entered the chamber where the other Elder 13 were waiting on him. Kevin as usual was greeted by Victoria and Kimberly. Victoria was a former Sector Six worker who never decided on a specific garment which would define her for the remainder of her time. She assumed that her life gathering food supplies for a century and a half, made her want to simply wear something called a "sundress" This was an antique style of clothing that was made from a synthetic substance which was intended to resemble something called "cotton" but it was very nice on her. It was usually full of the same botanistic relics which resided upon Kevin arms, but these were not dark, everything was light. Very small straps came over her slender shoulders to hold the dress up, but Kevin paid no attention to Victoria's attire.

Kimberly on the other hand was stunning in her ritualistic attire, a long flowing red dress, with many layers, she had many styles of this but Kevin always found her look amazing, and from the time when Victoria originally explained what it was she was wearing. "You see, Kevin, This is a black bustle dress, it is an amazing piece of artistic clothing from so long ago. You begin with a corset and a lobster tail style bustle."

Kevin interrupted, "A what?"

Pointing at her dress she pointed out the two

pieces, and then continued, "In the front I have a fake front with buttons, lapels, and drapes, but it is tied in the rear. As for the dress it is just a full length dress which was made to not touch my actual body due to my petticoat." She lifted the bottom of her dress to reveal the stiff fabric used to hold the fabric away from her body.

Today she was wearing one that was a mostly red and black, secretly Kevin thought of Laura, with her fascination for these two colors, but Kevin did not remark upon this as he thought it would be rude. The three of them lined up and walked towards the lobby, along with a few assistants who did some of the same retirements, except they had no idea what any of the actual items on the menu entailed.

Arriving at the group, Kevin said, "Derrick, will you follow me?" Kevin waited until Derrick rose and walked towards him to walk back towards the office. "Good morning, Derrick; I am Kevin, and I will be helping you get ready to move to Sector Seven." Remembering the script he has been saying for years and years, Kevin barely had to think about what to say next. His screen told him what Derrick had done for the last portion of his life.

"Now you have spent the last one hundred and fifteen years as a raw material processor in Sector Four, is this correct?" Kevin asked.

"Well that is partially correct." Derrick replied.

"Perfect," Kevin continued and then stopped, "wait what? What do you mean partially correct?" This rarely happened; the screen never lied about what the profession of the person was. Everyone did the profession they were perfect for, and this person would be no different.

"I did other things than process raw materials while in Sector Four. I sometimes would pick up the raw material from the gathers in Sector Four. Sometimes I would even get to travel out of Sector Four to visit other gathers in Sector Six. Other times..." Derrick continued to speak until Kevin interrupted him in mid-sentence.

"...right, but your main career is raw material processor in Sector Four. I understand, that many people do much more than their primary job, and it sounds like your alternative sabbaticals sound like some great times, but I do not want you to miss your travel time to Sector Seven with us speaking for so long." Kevin politely said, and then followed with, "this is your two hundred and seventeenth name day?"

"Well that is totally correct but after so many years, I just stopped paying attention to my actual age. When I received the message, I just took it on faith that I had been doing my job for that long, and I had lived that long." Derrick started to speak and if it was not for Kevin raising his hand to silence him, he would have continued.

"Sounds like an interesting affair, you have indicated that you would like to stay in Sector Seven for a minimum of thirty-seven years, is this still correct?" Derrick nodded his head quickly up and down over and over again. "If you do not mind me asking, why thirty-seven years? That is a very odd number of years to request." Kevin inquired.

"It just felt right. In Sector Four there is an ancient story about the power of the number thirty-seven, and I just felt like it would be a good number to choose." Derrick explained.

"You are not married, is that also correct?" Kevin asked, and Derrick just nodded and shrugged his shoulders, so Kevin simply moved on to his least favorite part of the routine. "Great, now there is one last thing, before you leave, is there anything you would like to do on the day you arrive?" The screen appeared in front of Derrick, displaying all the options for what he could do once arriving in Sector Seven.

Derrick stared at the list as if he had never been given a choice in his whole worthless life. Several minutes passed before Derrick spoke. "There is so much to choose from, but I think the most interesting sounding thing to do is the fire swallowing performance."

Kevin looked very surprised, it has been years since he had been told to prepare this retirement. Derrick entered his choice on the screen, and Kevin stood up. The two walked down the hallway and made several turns. Then they came to a door labeled Sector Seven, and Kevin opened the door for Derrick. Derrick walked into a room with holograms of dancing men in white faces called clowns, then Derrick turned around and Kevin handed the clowns a flaming stick. The clowns started to torment and chase Derrick around the room, knowing that there would be no escape. Finally the main clown, wearing a large red painted on smile bared his sharp teeth and said, "Open up, I have a candy pop for you" as he shoved the flaming stick down Derrick's face.

Derrick's face started to turn red as the fire began to cook him from the inside out. After several moments of agony, he fell down shaking, when one

of the clowns erupted into a fire that engulfed
Derrick's body in a fiery inferno.

# FROM THE LOST TEXTS OF THE GRAND AUTHORS (AS ALWAYS THIS IS BELIEVED TO NOT BE THE ORIGINAL VERSION OF THE TEXT):

You're going to be Grand Ruler, just like you were promised. But I worry about whether or not you have what it takes to seize the Leadership. You are too full of the milk of human kindness to strike aggressively at your first opportunity. You want to be powerful, and you don't lack ambition, but you don't have the mean streak. The things you want to do, you want to do like a good man. You don't want to cheat, yet you want what doesn't belong to you. There's something you want, but you're afraid to do what you need to do to get it. You want it to be done for you.

# MICHAEL

"What kind of people are we?" Michael yelled at Luke as they took the evening's sustenance in a private room on the top floor of the Hall of the Future.

"Where is this coming from?" Luke asked as he put his napkin down.

"You know where this is coming from; it is coming from the fact that we are the evil of the world. I read that old book you suggested. You know the one that used to have all the answers. And WE are the evil of the world. WE are the creatures of destruction." Each time Michael said we, he raised his voice to put further emphasis and he pointed violently at the door to the lounging area.

Luke only stared at Michael, which only served to enrage Michael more. "You used to care. I did some reading about what your people were like, and you were the good people of the world. You have been around the longest, and you seem to have no problem with what we do on a daily basis, you lie to people and put them through one standard unit of torture where they end up with an imagined

immortality, while I have the other job of ending their life in an impossibly evil way over and over again.
 You are evil for playing George, and I am evil for being a murderer."

"First, calm down Michael. It is just the two of us, you have no one to impress, and your actions will not serve to impress me. Second, I do not lie to anyone, while they do have the ability to not expire of old age, I do tell everyone that if they are in some sort of accident which would render anyone expired they will expire, which is what you provide. Would you suggest that we go back to overpopulation? Would you have us have the class system where some people do not receive the adequate amount of daily sustenance? Would you have the crime rate rise again?" At that last point, Michael tilted his head in confusion.

"Oh, that's right, you don't know about crime. So all your research failed to help you see the good we do. Crime is what we used to call it when people did any sort of action against another person or the governing body which was not allowed. This is an idea that is pretty much done away with, because of the system which has been around for so long.
 Society expands and contracts as we, the Elder 13, decide it needs to expand. Do not presume to judge me, or the work I have done over the years."

Michael sat silently and listened to the rebuke he was receiving, but inside he knew the decision he was about to make was correct. "Your right Luke. I apologize for my actions and vocalizations and my accusations. All is still not right, and I can no longer do this anymore." Michael allowed for the pause to hold before finishing his thought, "I would like to be released from my duties. I do not require another duty, I just want to die."

Luke quickly corrected Michael's major error, "No one dies; they expire or retire."

"No" Michael quickly countered, and began raising his voice, "they die. Call an A.S.P.S. an A.S.P.S. people die, and we are the cause. I want to die, and I want you to sign the order allowing it."

Luke sat silently for a long while, until quietly saying, "Then I can do nothing. I can only sign an order for a member of the Elder 13 to retire." With that, Luke stood up and walked out the door into the lounge.

"Well I guess the conversation is over" Michael spoke aloud to himself. Looking around the room, Michael started to feel that uncommon feeling of anger rise in his breast; however, tears fell quickly from their ducts.

Aloud Michael spoke, "I just don't understand. Just let me die. Who in George's name does he think he is to tell me I cannot die? I should have died many years ago, but no I was asked to join the Elder 13."

Around three hundred years ago, Michael on his two hundred and seventeenth name day arrived at the Hall of the Future and met with Max, the former Elder 13 member, who was wearing a traditional Japanese kimono. This was an odd style for anyone to adopt, as it was an set of robes and short pants in a Japanese style, but without the artwork. It was just bright green, at least on that day, years later when asked why he wore this he said, "It is a thing to wear."

Max informed Michael that he was selected

for a rare opportunity to move up in the government instead of retiring. Walking towards Michael, Max, wearing his Green kimono, said, "Michael" and Michael rose from his chair to follow Max towards his office, the office Frederick now used. As they entered the office, Max said, "Good morning, Michael; I am Max, and I will be helping you get ready to move to Sector Seven, or you have a second option, but we will get to that in a moment." Michael sat there and just nodded, as Max continued, "You have spent the last one hundred and fifty-six years in the Information Department, but you never rose very high, is that correct?"

Michael nodded his head again, and said, "They never understood my ideas. I was trying to dig through the misinformation and find the George honest truths. So I never reached very high."

Max nodded his head, and then started his pitch, "Just to make sure, this is your two hundred and seventeenth name day?" Michael dipped his head. "Perfect, now if you want your man retire to Sector Seven, and live your life in relaxing retirement, or you can pass up retirement and find all the truths you want."

Michael spoke the words, the words which have been troubling him for so many years after, "Let's find the truth."

As Michael came out of his daze, Richard was sitting there, in his black suit looking at Michael with utter disdain. "Why would you want to leave this? We have everything you want, everything you need, and you are above the law. If you want to bend Susan over and have a sexual encounter, you can, and she will let you, just for George's sake, stop trying to head down the path you are on. I will arrange Susan to descend to your floor tonight so she can take your mind off your current issues. No one will know about it except the three of us."

Michael stood up, "Do what you want Richard, but I am set in my decision, I will receive my departure, I will retire, and no amount of women or men sent to my floor will change my mind." With this Michael walked out of the room, towards the lift, and descended towards his floor.

# FROM SECTOR ONE GRAND WIRELESS SERVICE:

A message from the Hall of the Future: Please do not be late for your appointment, whenever summoned. You have been waiting two hundred seventeen years for this day; don't waste any time getting what you truly deserve.

# RICHARD

Hanging upside down five meters from the side on his floor of the Hall of the Future, Richard was finishing his daily exercise, but this cool down was the best part. Looking down at all the ants which would soon meet their destiny and fulfill their worthless life with their demise. They all believe they are important, but importance only comes from power, and Richard knows he has the ultimate power.

One standard unit later, Richard, dressed in his suit, today with his brand new ghost-white shirt. Richard felt great anger towards the rest of the Elder 13 for not recognizing the different shades of his shirts; they all lacked the full intelligence of the color spectrum to see what is before them. This is why he should be in charge, at least in Richard's own mind.

Down in the lobby of the Hall of the Future, Richard saw his group for this morning, and a smile filled his face. One of the retirees was Richard's favorite type of victim. This morning, Victoria was giving the opening speech, in her normal attire of mini skirt and short top to allow for her midriff to be on displayed. Richard never got along with Victoria, but never had the same odd feelings he has for Alice. As Victoria walked back towards her office after the normal speech, Richard told one of the workers, that he would be taking a specific retiree first.

Victoria went first, her short dress swayed as she walked towards the group and returned with her first for the day. Alice went next, and if it was possible, her shorts were shorter than usual. Richard stared at her arse as she walked away, hypnotized by the movements, and then as she returned Richard could do nothing but stare at bouncing breast that looked at every step to want to slip through the hole in the middle of her shirt. She was wearing nothing that would keep them in place, so Richard stared hoping for a slip to make his evil dreams come true. Richard wanted nothing better than to humiliate this low born trash by having her expose her unworthy flesh, and Richard would be able to drink up the vision and embarrassment of the humiliation of his lesser.

Richard waited a while until he decided to go get his specific person, allowing himself to cool his blood after that trashy temptress Alice raised it. After his temperature died off, Richard walked over the lobby and asked "Johnny" to follow him. When Johnny and Richard sat down in Richard's office, Richard started his normal routine.

"Good morning, sir; I am Richard, and I will be helping you get ready to move to Sector Seven. Before I start, I want to say what an honor it is to have you sitting in my office. Your work governing the Sectors is very impressive; I always enjoy meeting those who keep society in check."

Johnny, nodded his head and answered, "Well, Richard, was it?"

Richard nodded, "And still is."

"Well, I am ready for a vacation. The last ten years have been wonderful and so very stressful. You have no idea how hard it is making sure everything runs correctly every day."

Richard could only smile, but this statement chilled him to the soul, if Richard still has a soul. He wanted to stand up and explain the way things actually work, and that he is only the figure head. So he just continued with the formalities, "This is your two hundred and seventeenth name day? Is that correct sir?"

"While I suppose it is." Johnny scratched at his face while he thought back towards the past.

Richard was starting to get annoyed with all the talking Johnny was doing. Richard decided to press the issue to arrive at the fun part. "Great, you have indicated that you would like to stay in Sector Seven for at the minimum of forty years is this still correct?"

"I suppose a nice forty years vacation is in order after all I have kept society together for so long." Johnny would have continued if Richard did not place the screen in front of his stupid face.

"And you have done a wonderful job. You need to decide one thing before we are done. Is there anything you would like to do on the day you arrive?"

"Well, Richard," Johnny started, and at his name, Richard started to feel a hatred at this man he had not felt in many years. "I believe I want a little bit of it all." He started laughing.

Richard stood up, and Johnny followed, continuing to talk about his desire to become what would have been essentially referred to as a hedonist, as they walked towards the door. As he opened the door, Johnny walked through and entered a room with nothing except a chair. The door slammed behind Johnny causing him to jump, and he viewed Richard just standing there smiling, as he started to take off his black jacket.

"So, Johnny, you think you have any idea what it takes to run everything in the Sectors? You know nothing!" Richard yelled this last part, and pulled a knife from the wall and sliced Johnny's ear straight off the side of his head. Picking the ear off the floor, Richard started to speak into the ear in his hand, "Can you hear me now? Listen, you are puppet, you never did anything. None of you do. You only have power that We allowed you to have."

With this he grabbed his hand and broke all four of his fingers as they were bent backwards till the nail reached the wrist. Johnny started to cry and yelled, "I thought this was supposed to be my great retirement?"

Richard started to laugh and walked right up to Johnny's face and asked, "What you are not relaxed? Did you really think there was going to be a happy Sector Seven?" Richard closed in on his remaining ear and whispered, "Let me show you Sector Seven in all its glory," and with this, Richard carved a smile in Johnny's neck with his knife and blood started to flow like a fountain of red chocolate, which reminded Richard that he needed to have his midday sustenance with Luke today.

## FROM THE LOST TEXTS OF THE GRAND AUTHORS (AS ALWAYS THIS IS BELIEVED TO NOT BE THE ORIGINAL VERSION OF THE TEXT):

It's only your name that's my enemy. You'd still be yourself even if you stopped being a Stratford. What's a Stratford anyway? It isn't a hand, a foot, an arm, a face, or any other part of a man. Oh, be some other name! What does a name mean? The thing we call a red scent would smell just as sweet if we called it by any other name. Bill would be just as perfect even if he wasn't called Bill. Bill, lose your name. Trade in your name which really has nothing to do with you and take all of me in exchange.

# ALICE

Sitting in her accommodations, Alice heard her door open, knowing it was Richard, she simply asked, "Is everything in place?"

"What do you think?" Richard responded, and then Alice turned around to greet Richard in the way she had wanted to for years, since she learned the two of them had some of the same sick pleasures.

As Alice turned to face Richard, he turned and saw the female standing in front of him was not the low born girl he had hated for so long. She was wearing long red leather boots which went up to her thighs, a very short, all revealing red leather skirt which made it very clear she was not wearing any underwear, and a small red leather bra which completed the outfit.

"Do you like what you see?" she asked. Richard was completely taken off guard; he was not expecting this from Alice. They were just supposed to celebrate their plan.

"Yes," he replied to Alice, "you are a very good looking girl."

"Girl?" she said, "it has been a long time since anyone called me a girl! Well I like what I am seeing so my place is yours?" Richard was again taken back with the forwardness and aggressiveness of her approach; he was not used to thinking of her like this.

She took charge immediately, guiding him to a side door. Alice closed the door and told Richard to undress. Richard began to take off his suit and then she pushed him towards the bed and he fell backwards on to the bed.

"Look little Richard is waking up, we will soon see what you are capable of doing with it won't we?" Alice said to him, as Alice noticed his member. Alice took one of his hands and pulled it up towards the head of the bed, she took one leather cuff and tied his arm to the bedpost.

"What are you doing?" Richard asked, slightly panicked. He was not the one to ever be out of control.

"Hush! Quiet, let me do my stuff...you will like it, this will be an experience you will never forget." She chuckled as she took his other arm and tied that as well to the bedpost.

Now she bound his ankles to the other end of the bed with leather cuffs. Suddenly her voice changed, it became harsher, as hard as steel and cold as ice, "Now you are mine," she purred, "you cannot escape and I will do to you whatever I want. You still think I am piece of trash do you not?"

"Yes and this just further proves my thoughts were true. However, that does not mean I am not prepared to get into the gutter with you." It was not what she said but how she said it. Richard suddenly felt terrified, which was a feeling he had not felt in over two thousand years, he felt like a mouse must feel when confronted with a cat. She moved away from the bed to a cupboard and opened it. The cupboard contained a collection of what normally would be considered torture tools. An array of different whips, clamps, spikes, hoods, cuffs and things that Richard was sure she lifted from some of the Sector Seven rooms.

"What did I get myself into?" Richard asked. He tried to get loose, out of the cuffs, but that proved to not be possible.

Ignoring his question, Alice just noticed the struggle, and she yelled, "Yes, struggle, fight, I like it when my victims have a bit of life in them. The more you fight, the more you scream, the more pleasure you are going to give me. You worthless piece of excrement, you belong to me now!! You came to me voluntarily, you came to my room of your own free will, and you gave yourself to me of your own choice, now you are mine to do with whatever I want."

"No!!" Richard stated calmly. "I did not agree to whatever you have in mind"

Alice took a long nine tails whip out her cupboard. "I know you like to inflict pain, so do I. Let me see how you like taking some of the punishment, because you are going to feel a lot of pain before I am finished." Alice pulled her arm back and the whip landed with force on Richard's chest. The sharp pain silenced Richard and he only smiled back at her. "Yes, I thought you would like that. Now let's see how much pain you can take".

The whip descended again on Richard, leaving its mark on his chest. Something changed inside Richard, he did not feel the pain, only anger; anger at himself for waiting so long to meet with Alice, and anger at Alice keeping this a secret. All the misery he had gone through in his life, all the hardship, all the humiliation that had been building up during the years, the promotion he was not getting, the failure with this girl, everything was building up into an emotion which surpassed anger. The whip descended again and again, no sound came from Richard. Then the pain just became too much and the rage in him made him break the silence.

"Just wait until I get lose you Alice, I will let you eat that whip, I will break it on your back and then I will bring in a servant to snap their neck in two!!" Richard shouted in confused anger to Alice.

"And what makes you think that I will release you, little boy? I am going to have so much fun with you. This is for every time you treated me like less of a person because I came from a lesser group." Alice started to whip Richard again, harder and harder, whipping his chest, his stomach, and his legs. Richard could stand the pain and never let out a single shout of pain. This seemed to excite Alice more and she started to whip Richard even harder. She was whipping Richard so hard, blood started to be drawn; he had small wounds appearing all over his body. He was feeling more pain than he had thought was gone since he left the military. He was also losing his dignity and his anger at this low class wretch, Richard was could have started howling like an animal in pain but simply kept smiling. Alice stopped with her whip, she was breathing heavily from the exercise she had just gotten but also from the excitement she was feeling.

"Don't tell me you are getting tired already?" Richard mocked Alice once she stopped.

"I think I have warmed you up enough, it is

time for some real pain now, and I am going to enjoy this so much." Alice said. She turned her attention to her cupboard and after closely inspecting several items she took some clamps out of it and started to put them on Richard. The first one went onto his nipples. Richard was so excited from the whipping he did not even try to stop Alice, he just let it happen. Then the pain hit him, first it was a sharp pain, and slowly it started to dull out.

"Very good Richard, you are taking this like a good little boy. I now will start putting clamps on more painful places, can you guess where?"

"I am just looking forward to my turn." Richard said with a smile.

Alice did not even flinch she took her whip and started to whip Richard again, but without any effect. "I told you, you don't get a turn." Richard was beyond pain and in complete control. He showed her that the cuffs were off, and he was ready for his turn.

Alice was feeling panic now; this was not how she planned this out. She had played this game with several men and never had any been able to untie himself after she had started to play with them! Richard raised himself from the bed, blood dripping everywhere, he was bleeding from small wounds, and the clamp was still fixed to his nipple. He took a look at it and without even bothering to unclamp it he just tore it off his nipple. The pain it caused was just fuel to his still growing lust.

When Alice saw what he did she really started to panic, fear started to fill her and she started to back up against the wall. It was to no avail, slowly Richard walked towards her, and she had long, beautiful, red hair which Richard used to throw her on the bed.

"Undress," he ordered Alice, "you wanted to play? We'll play now, see how much pain you can take, see what happens when I break the whip on you and you start to bleed. I told you it was going to be my turn. You just would not listen to me."

Alice was too afraid to not obey, she undressed. She was a very beautiful woman with a very good figure. Against his better judgments she was arousing him. Richard bound Alice to the bed using the same cuffs which Alice tied him up. Alice had bound Richard belly up; he had felt more comfortable tying her belly down. Once she was tied, Richard was ready to start playing.

When he looked down at her he noticed something very queer, Alice had calmed down and her fear was gone. Richard took the whip that Alice had used on him and started to whip her with it, the snapping of the whip in the air, the sound of it on Alice's flesh was having a strange effect on Richard. Alice cried out in pain with every whiplash, but he hardly noticed that. The whip was hypnotizing him, the clapping, the sound it made on the flesh, the redness of her skin. It all reminded him of his time in the military getting information from those who did not want to tell him.

Still Richard was not really hitting Alice with his full force, something was holding him back. Maybe it was his upbringing, the morals he had been taught during his childhood, maybe it was just fear of letting himself go, but most likely it was the fear of liking too much what he was doing. Still a side of himself he had never explored before was starting to wake up, and slowly it was overtaking him. With every whiplash he was gaining force. Alice's back was turning bright red from the whip. Richard wanted to continue whipping Alice but his arm was getting tired, and he also wanted to do something else now. When he stopped whipping Alice he noticed she was weeping softly.

The weeping of Alice had a weird effect on Richard, it turned him on. For a moment he was not sure what to do now, he was being guided by something inside him, an instinct, and an emotion he had never felt before. He took another look inside the cabinet and found what he was looking for. He took a sharp knife and warmed the point with a small torch he had found in the cupboard, until it was glowing red.

For a minute Richard stopped to think of what he was about to do, did he really want to do this? Once done there would be no way he could undo it. It would mark him as much as it would mark her. Driven by an unnatural instinct, an inner force, some would call it a dark side; he let the point of the knife touch her flesh. Alice cried out in pain, there was no blood; the red glowing point of the knife had cauterized the wound. The smell of burning flesh filled his nostrils. Alice's cries of pain aroused him; he looked down at his crotch and noticed he was also enjoying this whole affair. The pain and control he was exerting over Alice was fulfilling a need in him.

Calmly, he lifted the knife and reheated it again. Her cries of pain would have melted the hardest of men, but it did not even bother him. The screaming of Alice had aroused Richard, he wanted more. He wanted both pain and pleasure at the same time. He drove the knife with force into the bedpost and pushed himself into her.

"I was right; you do like me, don't you?" Alice asked as she was being penetrated. "I will stay silent or scream depending on what you want. But I have an even better idea. Let's grab one of the servants."

Alice only smiled at the thought, so she pressed the button to summon one of the servants into her chamber, and a large male servant entered the door, and asked, "How may I help you?" It was obvious he was not pay attention to what was happening in the room or he would not have asked such a question.

The "helpless" Alice was trying desperately to free herself from the cuffs that bound her to the bed, as Richard just stood to the side looking out the window. The servant ran over to the bed to help Alice, and she kicked him in the head, knocking him into unconsciousness.

Alice stood up and crossed the room to meet Richard, they then started to take turns cutting pieces of the servant up, and licking the blood off of each other's bodies. "We must do this again, soon." Alice said.

# FROM THE LOST TEXTS OF THE GRAND AUTHORS (AS ALWAYS THIS IS BELIEVED TO NOT BE THE ORIGINAL VERSION OF THE TEXT):

In the beautiful city of Yorkshire, where our story takes place, a long-standing hatred between two families erupts into new violence, and citizens stain their hands with the blood of their fellow citizens. Two unlucky children of these enemy families become lovers and commit suicide. Their unfortunate deaths put an end to their parents' feud. For the next two hours, we will watch the story of their doomed love and their parents' anger, which nothing but the children's deaths could stop.

# LAURA

Standing in the mirror, Laura started to feel old. The years have gotten to her, and she could feel something bad was about to happen. This was not a new feeling, but it had been years since she felt anything like this, and that was when the vast execution of Sector Two and Sector Five, but that was so many years ago, that only eleven of the Elder 13 remember it, and no one else alive had any idea. But this time it felt much more personal, but Laura was quickly taken out of this premonition when she remembered she had to meet with Luke and Richard for midday sustenance.

Putting on her black yoga pants, and University shirt, she began to walk towards the lift and rose to the top floor. Walking past the main area, and into the private chamber in the rear, Laura walked right in and saw Luke just sitting thinking. Looking around to make sure they were alone, she said, "How's it going padre?" This was a long joke between the two of them, and was never said around anyone else, ever.

Years ago, when Laura first met Luke before their modification, she looked at the priest in front of her and just asked, "How's it going padre?" She was just a silly girl, who only remembered this part of the Church practice was to always call Priest's "father" but she always like what her roommate called hers, so she always did the same.

Raising his head, Luke said, "Laura, when are you going to stop calling me that?"

"When are you going to stop dressing like a priest? When are you going to stop using the rosary? When are you going to break your vows?" Laura asked, this series of questions was new, except for the last one.

"I have broken all but one, and that one I cannot imagine where to start." Luke started to laugh, because he knew what was going to come next.

"You see, you strip down, and stick it in. It is not that hard, well if it is hard it makes it easier." They both started to laugh. Laura remembered when she first found out that a few hundred years into their life together, before they even created the Elder 5, that while Luke agreed to break his vow of poverty, and his vow of charity came and went as was required, he would never break his vow of chastity. This was one of the many secrets Luke and Laura kept between themselves.

"So you have told me. And I have watched many people over the years, but it is nothing I want to take part in. I am the oldest man alive." Luke trailed off at this statement, as it was something he did not like to talk about. While Laura and Luke were the oldest in terms of time modified, Luke was still twice Laura's age at the time of modification. While now this did not even seem like a second of time, the look of the two of them always bothered him.

"Why are we meeting today?" Laura asked, ending the playful conversation, and getting down to business.

"Let me finish my routine please; O my Jesus, forgive us our sins, save us from the fires of hell, lead all souls to Heaven, especially those who have most need of your mercy." Luke finished his ancient ritual.

"Okay. You done? Why are we meeting today?" Laura asked, for a second time.

"We have a great problem brewing; Richard just retired the most recent Ruler." Luke said with a worried tone.

"I just assumed we were going to talk about Alice's retirement, and her other activities."

"One problem at a time." Luke said, finishing the conversation, and the two sat in silence until Richard entered the room.

Richard entered with a flourish, and bowed at the waist, when he greeted Luke. "Luke, I hope George is smiling on you." Noticing Laura on the other side of the table, Richard nodded and said, "And I see Laura will be joining us." The venom in his voice was noticeable to everyone, Laura and Richard did not get along, because Richard resented Laura for the history she and Luke had, a history he would never know.

"Please have a seat, Richard" Luke said with a small edge in his voice, Richard continued to stand in defiance. "Or just keep standing, it does not really matter. We are having a small bit of a problem, with you and the way you have been retiring people."

"How do you mean?" Richard asked with a raised eyebrow, "I have done everything by the rules.

I give the soon to retire the choice on first activity, then I take them to their room. So what is the issue?"

"The issue is Johnny." Laura yelled, then sat back down when Luke put his hand on her shoulder.

Richard looked with extreme anger at Laura, composed himself and answered, "He made his choice and I took him to his room. How was I to know that there was no cameras in that room. Must be an error." Richard smiled the most innocent smile he could muster.

Luke, with a raised eyebrow, answered slowly, "What makes you think there were no cameras?"

Richard smoothly responded, "When I was watching the replay, I could not find the video of that retirement."

Laura responded with repulsion in her voice, "Why would you re-watch the retirements? That is cruel."

Luke raised his hands again to silence everyone at the table, "Some cameras do not go towards the general archive, which is what you can replay, but everything is recorded." Luke paused for a long while, then "Even this room."

Richard started to perspire, and quickly asked, "What happens to those video feeds?"

"Only a few people have access to those holos, and Laura and I are two of them. So we have some issues with the way you retired Johnny, and we are going to talk about it."

# FROM SECTOR ONE GRAND WIRELESS SERVICE:

A message from The Grand Ruler, Michael Hollow: Since Grand Ruler Johnny Whiteneck has stepped away, we must remember that with new personal comes new challenges. My various assistants have informed me that we are looking forward to another great and wonderful decade of prosperity, as long as nothing goes wrong.

# RICHARD

Richard was perspiring as he learned that everything was being recorded, and even in the rooms that for the last few hundred years he knew were not, were. Trying to play the new situation without worry Richard asked, "What happens to those video feeds?"

"Only a few people have access to those holos, and Laura and I are two of them. So we have some issues with the way you retired Johnny, and we are going to talk about it."

Oh course, Richard thought, Laura and Luke would have the secret access to all the extra bits of fun he had been having and just now decided to say something. When did Luke get wise to what was going on under his rule? What will Luke do?

Richard started to think back to when he was first asked to join the Elder 5, which soon after him joining they took some of the power away by making it the Elder 7. Richard upon receiving his modification joined the military of the United European Kingdoms to rid the Earth of those who would not fall in line. He quickly rose to the level of High Strategist and the lofty rank of General.

Richard was summoned back to the
Kingdoms, where he was going to meet with the
Grand Ruler. Deciding to not wear his military
uniform, Richard decided to wear his nicest black suit,
and he walked to the Hall of Might, the place where
the Ruler kept, when he was placed into a dark room,
Richard stood for several standard units until finally a
door on the other side opened, and Richard without
prompting walked through, and found four men and
women sitting in the five chairs prepared around a
table.

Once more without prompting, Richard sat at
the empty space and did not speak, until the one who
must of been in charge, as his garish outfit of all red
flowing robes spoke volumes on how important this
man thought he was. Richard never thought he
needed any type of wonderful attire to show how
great he is, anyone who was in a room with him
instantly knew that this was the man not to cross.

They explained that they were the part of the
real ruling government of the world, and they would
like him to join their ranks, and help run the United
European Kingdoms and hopefully one day, all of
earth. Richard listened to the specifics, and agreed, he
would never have made it to his summons, and
people would mourn the loss of his greatness, but
now he would be ready to make real changes. Soon
after he joined, the Elder 5 turned into the Elder 7
when Susan, the woman who used her body to get
anything she wanted in life. Richard did not dispute
that it was an amazing body, and the dresses she
wore, did nothing but make the body look even
better. Richard knew he would run this group, and
bring it back down to a reasonable size one day, but

he would plan it out perfectly.

Over a thousand years later, Richard pressed for Alice, a lower stationed nobody, to join the group and he made his first real move towards his inevitable takeover. Richard had no doubt that the meeting he was now sitting in would also eventually go his way. He just had to remember his main rule.

Looking up at the two across from him, Richard slowly raised his head looking calm and asked simply, "And what would you like to discuss? What is it you think you saw?" Richard decided his best course of option was to double down and call Luke's bluff. Hundreds of years ago, Richard started to do some research into the life of Luke and Laura's life before the grand experiment, and did not find out much he could use. Laura was a student, and Luke was something called a Cardinal.

Using the knowledge he possessed about the past, Richard started the attack, "It was no worse than what your kind used to do in your former profession." Richard read about how Cardinals who were leaders of something called a "Church" who used to have illegal and unauthorized sexual encounters with under aged persons. While Luke may not have taken apart of it, be must have known someone. Turning to Laura, "Or what your kind used to do in the dungeon rooms?" His research showed that people in university lived in dungeon rooms with a roommate and would have multiple unauthorized sexual encounter with multiple persons a night, while cheating on the test.

Shaking her head, Laura replied, "Richard, as much as you try, you will never understand what it was like back then. Luke was a respected man of the cloth, and I was a college student who had just moved from a bad place and lucked out. But you will not get us to stop talking about you to speak on us."

"Thank you Laura," Luke replied calmly, "but I do not think that is the point Richard was trying to make." Uncrossing his arms, opening them in a full spread, Luke softly spoke, "Ask what you will, say what you must, but we will get to what we need to know before the day ends, and the day shall only end when I say it ends."

Unbuttoning his jacket, Richard began to sit down again, preparing for what may. "What do you have to say?"

"Simply this, your actions are cruel, your methods are barbaric, and it shall not be endorsed any longer. You slip up once more, you shall be expelled from the Elder 13 and it will cause unbalance in society. A society you proclaim to love."

Richard sat for a few moments before opening his mouth to respond, "How do I respond to such an threat? My job is to retire the members of our society who reach their two hundred and seventeenth name day. They do not go to a Sector Seven. For George's sake, our Sector Seven monitors do not even turn on, except to watch replays. Why does it matter how they end their worthless lives? Why not have it entertain me? And more to the point why do the ritual of having them picked, or even going through the motions of making it seem like they may reunite with family?"

Laura stood up and started to raise her voice, "Because it cruel to end someone's life that way. As for the ritual, it is to keep people unaware what will happen." Luke raised his hand to silence her.

"The ritual is to keep the truth silent. You are correct in this, but it is so chaos does not grab our society. I do not care about watching the replays, but it should not entertain you, it should do nothing to you. It is just a service to our community, nothing more, nothing less."

Sneering Richard began to speak again, "Really? A community service? Just like when we got rid of all the members of every other Sector except ours. Where was your infinite compassion there? Where was the care for their lives then? You gave the order, who are you to decide what is wrong and what is right?"

Silence fell over the room as Richard sat back down, and Luke just sat thinking. This silence remained uninterrupted until Michael burst in the door saying, "You must come with me, and it is Edward."

# FROM THE LOST TEXTS OF THE GRAND AUTHORS (AS ALWAYS THIS IS BELIEVED TO NOT BE THE ORIGINAL VERSION OF THE TEXT):

You can't eat human flesh, but if it feeds nothing else, it'll feed my revenge. He's insulted me and cost me greatly. Because I'm a Jets. Doesn't a Jets have eyes? Doesn't a Jets have hands, bodily organs, a human shape, five senses, feelings, and passions? Doesn't a Jets eat the same sustenance, get hurt with the same weapons, and warm up in summer and cool off in winter just like a Sharks? If you prick us with a pin, don't we bleed? If you tickle us, don't we laugh? If you poison us, don't we die? And if you treat us badly, won't we try to get revenge?

# EDWARD

Sitting on the bed, Edward was replaying the last few conversations he has had with the rest of the Elder 13. The realization that the others do not take his contributions seriously because he was so young, but he was not young. He was old enough to do what he wanted with his life. He wanted to retire, he wanted to die, and he wanted someone to care. Richard was right, it would take a great act to make anything change, and he was the perfect one to start it all off.

"I wonder if Richard would do it for me." Edward said aloud, but then thought about the response Richard would have if he asked. Would he be glad to help end his life? Would be even agree? Would he prolong the suffering? Would Alice do a better job? Could he just go to the BBQ area of Sector Seven and finish himself off?

"I will do it myself, but first I will write an official document that will expose us all." Edward started to dictate his message, and when he was finished, he set it up to hang over his body for one hour after he is found, but then to be sent to every person's monitor and this hopefully would get the message out. The truth must be sent out, and Edward knew he would be the sacrificial lamb.

Sitting on his bed, he began to strip off his clothing, and put on the traditional jumpsuit of the society, and walked over to his closet. He pulled out a sword, which he stole from the Sector Seven Medieval Room, and stabbed himself in the stomach.

Life started to pass from Edward's body, as he flung himself out of the window of his accommodations and landed on the way to the walkway pavement in front of the Hall of the Future Edward started to think about all that has happened.

Edward remembered meeting Luke when he was first modified on his twenty-fifth name day. He was not modified by Luke but by some random person who then sent him to the next room for placement. Edward was chosen to be a member of the media elite. He would cover the topics which concerned the people in the Sectors of the United European Kingdoms.

Edward did not want to do anything chasing after the government, until one day there was a tip about a group calling themselves the Watchers, who were convinced there was a secret government above the one we all knew about. When Edward refused to look into this conspiracy, he was forced out of his job and was sentenced to death for leading a mutiny against the government.

It was in the jail awaiting his own death that Richard first approached him to join the same organization he was told to look into. Edward took it and now it was Richard's idea to make a large statement, which he would by placing himself as a fallen hero.

Edward met with the walkway and his body liquefied leaving only a mess with a virtual message hovering above his body:

## The Truth from the True Ruling Body of The Sectors

My name is Edward, and I died over five hundred years ago, but today you get to see my body. I am a member of the ruling group called the "Elder 13" which has been actually ruling for thousands of years, even several of the original members are still ruling. We prop up the Grand Leadership, including the Grand Ruler.

My job was to help retire those unfortunate bodies who did not meet their end before their two hundred and seventeenth name day, where the realization of Sector Seven would finally be realized. The only issue with this is there is no such thing. To make matters worse, all six of the Sectors used to be filled with people and buildings much like Sector One, but because of an uprising they were dispatched without any record. I am creating this spectacle so for a short while, people will know the truth, and hopefully a real reform will occur.

Sector Seven is the chambers we place the individuals who arrive for their retirement on their two hundred and seventeenth name day, but we murder them. We roast them alive, stab them with metal, force them to fall off tall buildings, much like I just did, and many worse fates. I have participated in this slaughter of you lambs for long enough, but I shall not be a part of it any longer. I ask you all to look into the records and find me, find record of the other Sectors and what they were like before we took their population and displaced them into the void to which I now find myself.

I end this death letter with simply this. How do you explain that the Grand Ruler wears the same outfit as the rest of you, but there are a dozen people who seem to wear whatever it is they would like, and no one ever questions them.

Please people open your eyes,

*Edward*

## FROM THE LOST TEXTS OF THE GRAND AUTHORS (AS ALWAYS THIS IS BELIEVED TO NOT BE THE ORIGINAL VERSION OF THE TEXT):

She would have died later anyway. That news was bound to come someday. Tomorrow, days creep slowly along until the end of time. And every day that's already happened has taken fools that much closer to their deaths. Life is nothing more than an illusion. Life is a story told by an idiot, full of noise and emotional disturbance but devoid of meaning.

# SUSAN

The door opened in Susan's quarters, and she knew the day had finally come for Michael would come into the door and take what he had been wanting for hundreds of years.  From behind his arm grabbed my wrap from off my shoulders and tossed it to the floor.

Susan had decided on the black crepe silk with the halter cut bodice. The collar was two inches high and covered in small burnished gold beads, so she did not wear any additional jewelry, but this did not mean she did not still wear her favorite amber drop earrings that seemed to compliment the dress and catch the light as they moved. The body was tailored to hug every curve and slit to mid-thigh in a daring attempt at sexy. The style of the dress left the shoulders and back bare, so Michael could see the slight scars on her back.

Susan began to think about how the different people she retired today looked at her.  There was something about moving through the crowd, knowing how little she was wearing, that was exciting to her. It was as though she had some delicious secret and wore a mischievous smile with the great knowledge that the those looking at her, could not meet her eye,

Michael gaze raked over Susan's body in a leisurely assessment that sent her system on a slow burn. She could feel her skin ripple as though his eyes caressed its surface and caused her heart to flutter beneath her breast. All the lights extinguished and Michael seemed to disappeared as though he never existed, blending into the darkness. Susan blinked and felt herself shudder. Frowning she searches the darkness but there was no sign of him, causing her body to betray her as her nipples strain against the silk as though anticipating Michael's touch.

Susan's was trying to remember the last time she had had something even close to this strong reaction to a man, especially when he hadn't even laid a hand on her. Finally she saw his outline as he sat across the room from her. His grin was quick and infectious as I felt myself return it and Susan felt her legs go liquid. The deep timber of his voice made her chest tighten and mouth go dry.

He whispered softly, "I hope you won't report me tomorrow."

Susan only smiled and started to turn when his hands settled at her waist, drawing her back against him preventing the movement. The feel of his hard body pressed against hers from behind was enough to cause her throat to tighten and only the sultry response of "Only if you do it right." forced out in a soft throaty whisper.

Susan could feel her heart beat against my ribs like a bird caught in a cage and could hear the smile in his words. Michael may not of known what he was doing to her, but she liked it regardless. She started to prepare herself as she rubbed her arse against him, feeling him swell and grow hard as his fingers traced the soft curve of her spine, conveniently left bare by the cut of this dress.

Michael laugh was deep and soft against Susan's ear before his lips touch her bare shoulder. Then the air was cool against her skin as he moved away, gone before she could steady her nerves enough to turn and look. Susan felt her nipples grow taunt and fevered as his slow motions forced her to wait for what they both wanted.

The two of them were in the sleeping quarters, and Susan found herself being lifted as she was forced against the wall and was lifted upwards. His thigh pressed between hers lifted her onto her toes as his hands gripped my wrists pinning them to the wall. Susan could barely breath and the uncontrolled lust in his eyes was reflected in mine. He took my mouth roughly. Desire like a demand as his tongue parted her lips. She met his need with my own, heated and urgent as their tongues explored and coaxed the flames higher between us. His hands moved up over her bare arse, drawing the lower part of the dress up around my waist to free her legs. He didn't have the time to remove her underclothing, as an alarm was sounded, forcing the two of them to quickly part, and look at the monitor to see a body falling from the top of their tower.

Michael and Susan both groaned as they realized that their desires would not be fulfilled until another day because an emergency happened. Susan deeply kissed Michael one last time before they both knew they would have to descend to the walkway to handle what was next, As the two kissed, Susan felt him release her lips as his mouth moved lower over her throat and down to seize her nipple through the silk. The pleasure was enough to make Susan think about not leaving the room, but she picked his head away from her nipple, and said, "To be continued."

# FROM THE LOST TEXTS OF THE GRAND AUTHORS (AS ALWAYS THIS IS BELIEVED TO NOT BE THE ORIGINAL VERSION OF THE TEXT):

You rebels! Enemies of the peace! Men who turn their weapons against their own neighbors they won't listen to me? You there! You men, you beasts, who satisfy your anger with fountains of each other's' blood! I'll have you tortured if you don't put down your swords and listen to me. Three times now riots have broken out in this city, all because of a casual word from you. Everyone else, go away for now. As for the rest of you, I'll say this once more: go away or be put to death.

# LAURA

Leaving one room, to go out in the open, was a shock to Laura's system. The outside did not always agree with the Elder 13, as their dress was vastly different from the rest of society, but Laura hoped that the difference in appearance would not be commented on. Laura was both relieved and repulsed as she arrived at the Sector of walkway where Edward's body was lying looking like a pavement creature which had been just placed under a grounded A.S.P.S. the force pressed all Edward towards his outside, and Laura looked at the lifeless immortal and realized they were only twelve members now in the Elder 13.

Within a standard unit, the remaining eleven members came to look at the lifeless body of the Elder they had dismissed so often. When Alice came upon the body, she only smiled at the sight of the liquefied body on the walkway, turned and walked back indoors Hall of the Future with a slight lift in her step. Richard walked towards the body, knelt down smiled and just stared at the liquid.

"Why are you smiling?" Luke asked Richard.
"Why do you think I am smiling Luke?

Laura? You have watched my retirement holos, you really think I don't see a beauty in what Edward just went through, you have really lost your way."

"His way? Our way?" Laura started to let loose the full force of her fury at Edward, reminding him that this will bring instability to the Elders. It will bring further scrutiny towards who really runs the government, as how will the Grand Ruler explain how someone who was born over two hundred and seventeen years ago, just now ended up on the walkway in front of the very place he is supposed to be processed into retirement; however, Luke spoke with his most powerful voice.

"This is not the place to have this conversation, I want the rest of you back in the building. As for Edward, we will do nothing."

"Nothing?" Laura exclaimed, "How can you, a man of the ancient faith say we should just leave Edward in the walkway without doing anything to help him?"

"Help him?" Luke said softly, "He is beyond my help, we must protect our current way of life and get ready for what is about to come."

At this, Laura knew the conversation was over, and she helped gather the rest inside the Hall of the Future, where they would wait on the top floor until Luke came to address the remainder of the Elder 13.

During the Lift ride, Susan and Michael began whispering to each other about the implication of only having twelve members in the Elder 13 again. Laura could not make out the rest of their whispered conversation, but the two of them started to put their hands on each other, making Laura start to feel embarrassed about her lack of a personal life. The closest thing she had to a lover, was the ultra-platonic relationship with a former Cardinal, who has still never broken his vow of celibacy, despite what happened so many years ago,

Several standard units expired until Luke rejoined the Elder 13 in the lounge where the other eleven were sitting watching the Sector One monitor.

# FROM SECTOR ONE GRAND WIRELESS SERVICE:

Every day is a new day for your life. Recently there have been reports of people rioting around the time of their two hundred and seventeenth name day, this is not true, and if it was to inspire you do anything, DON'T! This would bring a sudden shift of your retirement plans, and that would be a shame for all you wonderful citizens who have given so much to our society.

# LUKE

Standing on the walkway, the Grand Ruler walked towards the recent body of one of the actual rulers of society, Luke quickly walked away, knowing that his presence would only add more questions to the already odd investigation that was about to happen. Luke could not bring the Elder 13 into the spotlight, as it would take near five hundred years before the norm would return. Walking through the lobby of the Hall of the Future, Luke thought back the last few times they had been without a full thirteen membership, while those times were difficult, they were expected, as the Elder did the right thing and served their full term, and only after securing a replacement were they allowed to retire.

Luke boarded the lift to go and speak with the rest of the Elder 13 who had no doubt gathered on the top floor's lounge waiting for him as he remembered that near a thousand years ago when the last leader of the Elders passed away leaving Luke in charge and the chaos this caused. Luke was elected as the next leader, a honor he did not want again, but once again he was thrust into leadership. The responsibilities of leading everyone is why he stopped leading when the group grew to its level of thirteen. When it was decided to grow to this larger number, while not being the first increase, Luke did not like the idea of adding more people to this group, but spearheaded by Richard, it became so.

Even before this though, Luke remembered the first time he was asked to be in charge of the Elder 5. Mara, the teacher, suggested that Luke be the leader of the group they just created to help the combining world government deal with any issues, and separating the land masses into Sectors with resources being pooled together unlike any time in the history of Earth. Laura, the Environmental Toxicologist, and Sebastian, the Engineer, helped with the division and the divide of labor, but mostly they helped convince Johnston, the Doctor, to allow for Luke, the Cardinal, the lead.

Johnston always believed that because he was the most educated of the five, he should be in charge, but it was Mara who reminded the group that the one who least wants to lead, but can still lead, should lead. This is how Luke became in charge, even after reeling from his most recent loss; which he refused to discuss with any of the Elder 5.

Hundreds of years later, they decided to expand the group to seven, so they could easily push through when one of them decided they have had enough life, as Johnston did fifty years into the first full cycle of modification. Johnston was replaced with a brilliant military strategist named Richard. The expansion also allowed for Susan, the government spokeswoman, and the late Walter another physician joined the Elder 7. But it was at this increase Luke decided to allow for Sebastian to take the reins of leadership.

The lift stopped, and Luke stepped over the threshold to see the remaining Elder 13 looking at him for the answer of what to do next. This was the first time in most of these Elder's memories that an Elder did not just find their replacement and then retire. But Luke knew Laura, Susan, and Richard would remember Leslie of the Elder 11 era taking her life in much the same way Edward just did, leading to the promotion of Alice into their ranks and the expansion once again into adding another two members. Luke had to insure that the number would not rise again.

"I am sure you have many questions," Luke started, when he was quickly stopped by Alice.

"Yes, oh grand leader, please comfort us, just as you had so many other time," the sarcasm in her voice was so thick. Turning to a serious tone, "I think what we need to do is replace him, and maybe even add some members of this group. There is precedence of doing just that, but mainly I would like to know how we are going to fix this situation. I mean there was the note.

Luke read the note several times before leaving Edward on the walkway trying to figure out what to do with the information presented. "We can do nothing about the letter." Luke declared, "If we do anything it proves the letter is correct, and that would cause everything to come down. We will not expand our members, and we will find a replacement for Edward soon."

"Let's not replace him," Richard spoke out, "he was just slowing down, and I know most of you do not remember how wonderful it was to have less members. I would say no offence, but I truly do mean to offend some of you."

"Richard, you are not helping the situation, just let Luke figure out what is best." Laura spoke up.

"Do not presume to speak to me that way Laura, you may have been doing this for a long time, but so have I. I will not be spoken down to by someone like you."

Luke spoke loudly, "Enough! Everyone back to their accommodations. For the next few days we will let the workers fill in for us; those being retired, will be simply taken to a BBQ, and those being modified will just have to live without us helping them through all their questions. We will be out of touch until we can speak with the Grand Leadership and the Grand ruler to help them. That is what we are actually tasked with. All depart!"

As the Elder 13 all left towards the lift; Richard, Alice, and Laura stayed behind. Richard spoke once the space was empty, save for them, "You need to take action Luke and you know it."

"Laura and Luke, maybe your time has come to leave the area and retire." Alice added.

"Richard, I have dealt with you for so many years, I will not deal with your strategy ideas today; Alice I never want your counsel, I know the two of you are plotting something, or maybe you just enjoy the evil ways of the world together, but I want you both to leave and go back to your accommodations."
As Richard and Alice left, Laura looked over at Luke and he simply shook his head and she left him alone.

## FROM SECTOR ONE GRAND
## WIRELESS SERVICE:

It has been weeks since anyone has heard from the leaders of "The Watched." When asked, no one really remembers what it was they stood for. The Grand Ruler said that this group never existed really, and was just made by some trouble makers trying to get their name in print.

# LUKE

Standing looking into the looking glass, Luke noticed Laura standing behind him; "What is it Laura?" Slightly annoyed.

"I wanted to ask what you think we should do." Laura asked looking the same as she always did with her Texas Tech Sweater. "Do you think Richard had anything to do with this death?"

"Yes. Do you ever read the Grand Announcement? The one with the 'Grand Authors,' do you remember these text?" Luke asked.

"I know they are not read anymore, and once during University I had to read the original author, but I don't remember too much about it. Why is this relevant? How does this pertain to the situation at hand?" Lara asked.

"All the world's a stage, and all the men and women merely players. They have their exits and their entrances, and one man in his time plays many parts, his acts being seven ages. At first the infant, mewling and puking in the nurse's arms. Then the whining schoolboy with his satchel and shining morning face, creeping like snail unwillingly to school. And then the lover, sighing like furnace, with a woeful ballad made to his mistress' eyebrow. Then a soldier, full of strange oaths and bearded like the part, jealous in honor, sudden and quick in quarrel, seeking the bubble reputation even in the cannon's mouth. And then the justice, in fair round belly with good capon lined, with eyes severe and beard of formal cut, full of wise saws and modern instances; and so he plays his part. The sixth age shifts into the lean and slippered pantaloons with spectacles on nose and pouch on side, His youthful hose, well saved, a world too wide for his shrunk shank, and his big manly voice, Turning again toward childish treble, pipes and whistles in his sound. Last scene of all, that ends this strange eventful history, is second childishness and mere oblivion, sans teeth, sans eyes, sans taste, sans everything. Have you ever heard it told that way?" Luke asked.

"Never, it was always easier speech, and they were not ages, they were parts, and something about actors, not players. It was not nearly this difficult of a speech, but what does this have anything to do with anything?" Laura asked, she was starting to get annoyed with the whole idea of long quotations.

"The end of days is coming, Richard and Alice are going to try to recreate something I have been fearing for years. Since, well since that specific time." Laura knew what he was referring to, but it was never spoken between the two of them. "We are the in the second childishness right now, we have lost the taste of our purpose, we have lost our teeth, and soon we will lose our sight, but all that we have now and we shall have it soon for no longer."

"Is this from one of the old books? Your old books?" Laura asked impatiently. "What are we going to do about the crisis we find ourselves in now?"

"Nothing. We must retract from everything in society. We must withhold until everything calms back down. Did you ever read the story about the animals who took over the farm?" Luke asked.

"No, and I do not care. I care about what has just happened today." Laura rose her voice.

"Hold your temper. The point of the story is that as the leadership changes, society; that is the society who runs everything, the workers; never notice the change. Life continues as it always has for them," Luke calmly replied.

"So you are saying, we do nothing, because it will not do anything, or are you saying we are the workers, or are we the rulers I have always thought we are? Your riddles make less and less since. I am going to go and end this now. I will override the controls of their accommodations and turn off the air." Laura stood to leave.

"Do not go towards that path my darling. That path will only lead towards your own damnation. Do not go towards the same path that has swallowed Alice and Richard, you are better than they are." Luke stood straight up and felt like he had so many years ago that he forgot that he had that voice. After several moments Luke sat back down and said, "I apologize for speak to you in that way. I am just so shaken about what has happened, that I slipped into those old ways."

"Are you ever going to tell me what happened?" Laura asked, already knowing the answer.

The two sat quietly for near on a standard unit

until Laura stood and excused herself.  Luke did not even nod, he just sat thinking.

# FROM SECTOR ONE GRAND WIRELESS SERVICE:

Yesterday a mad man known as Edward through himself off of the Hall of the Future just shy of his two hundred and seventeenth name day. There has been vast rumors that the body contained a note for everyone that took aim at the Grand Ruler. To squash all these rumors the Grand Wireless Service has obtained a copy of the note, and will publish it in its full form here.

### The Truth

My name is Edward, and I am a member of the group called the Watchers which has been trying to find the truth about who really rules. The Grand Leadership, including the Grand Ruler has tried to shut my group up in many ways.

My job was to try to get close to those who work in the Hall of the Future, to uncover the truth about Sector Seven. After years of work, I have only found one thing, Sector Seven is the greatest place, and the thing that keeps the Grand Ruler up at night, is he must wait until his two hundred and seventeenth name day to go and retire there.

I end this death letter with simply this. I have been wrong and so have the rest of the Watchers, and if any of them find this note, please do not travel the same path as I have.

Please people open your eyes,

*Edward*

# ALICE

Alice stood looking down at the walkway that Edward had just flung himself from what a waste of a person she thought to herself. An opening of the door startled Alice into bringing up a defensive stance. She saw that it was Richard and she slowly dropped her stance and asked, "What are you doing here?"

"I was looking for another go around, but I suspect what will end up happening is for us to discuss the next part of the plan." Richard sat down in the chair provided upon him entering her accommodations.

"This was your plan, I wanted nothing to do with it; but I suspect I have no other choice but to help you now. As for another go around, I could always take another portion, but first we need to decide which we will keep."

"Leave that to me" Richard replied as he started to walk towards Alice. "We have taken care of Edward."

"You. You have taken care of Edward." Alice quickly corrected.

"Edward has been taken care of, how is that? We cannot risk losing neither Luke nor Laura, but I think we can take a special revenge on them. I think Susan and Michael could be fun to keep around, maybe we could watch their 'will they, won't they' closer."

"You really think they haven't yet? Also it is too risky to keep Luke and Laura around, they will stop us, and I don't care how perfect your plan is. Who will be the last one? Victoria? Kimberly? Or do you want to keep one of the males like Marcus?" Alice asked, remembering the day when the Sector Two and Sector Five disappeared.

"Marcus thought I was too extreme on the day we wiped out those two Sectors."

"It is funny, I was just thinking about that day, and while he was correct, it was extreme, he has done a great job retiring people in the evening almost as good as we do. As for finishing what we started, how about upon conclusion of the plan we will wait until then I'll keep the knife in the fire." Alice said with a smile as she closed the door leaving Richard on the other side.

# FROM THE LOST TEXTS OF THE GRAND AUTHORS (AS ALWAYS THIS IS BELIEVED TO NOT BE THE ORIGINAL VERSION OF THE TEXT):

Now is the spring of our discontent, and all of my family's troubles have come to a glorious end, thanks to my brother. All the clouds that threatened the Lancaster family have vanished and turned to sunshine. Now we wear the wreaths of victory on our heads. I was badly made and don't have the looks to strut my stuff in front of pretty sluts. I've been cheated of a nice body and face, or even normal proportions. I am deformed, and so badly formed that dogs bark at me as I limp by them. I'm left with nothing to do in this weak, idle peacetime, unless I want to look at my lumpy shadow in the sun and sing about that. Since I can't amuse myself by being a lover, I've decided to become a villain. I've set dangerous plans in motion, using lies, drunken prophecies, and stories about dreams to set one against another.

# SUSAN

Unease was causing Susan's skin to create goose pimples all over her body, but this was a time that the chill of the Hall of the Future's accommodation had nothing to do with. A standard unit ago, Richard contacted her to descend to the lobby of the Hall of the Future to have a meeting called by Luke. Sitting in her lounger, Susan asked herself the obvious questions: Why didn't Luke contact her himself? Why is the meeting down the lift, and not up?

Thinking it was better to just follow orders, she dressed herself and prepared to descend, when Laura came to speak with her. Appearing at the lift door, Laura, dressed in her University shirt and yoga pants, looked like a young girl, even as she is far older than Susan herself is. Allowing Laura entrance they sat down in the main room of Susan's accommodations.

Susan asked, once the two were seated, "Why are we having this meeting? And why is it in the lobby?"

Laura, sitting with her legs crossed, simply

sighed and responded, "I do not know. Luke did not tell me anything, and he was more interested in pontificating towards me. Referencing old books of authors no one cares for, and even getting the quotes wrong."

"What do you think about Edward?"

Sitting silently for several moments, Laura again spoke carefully, "I think it is tragic, but I think there is more to this than what is evident."

"What makes you think that?"

"Something my father told me, before he died." Laura started, realizing that Susan had no idea what she was talking about. "You know that I was one of the original five persons selected to be modified so many centuries ago." Laura paused. "As was Luke."

"Wait, so you were around before all this came about?" Susan asked quickly.

"Yes, and it was a different time back then, people were much different. Society was getting out of control and five people were chosen to be part of an experiment. It was to see if the world could sustain itself with less people, if those people lived longer, and never passed their prime." Laura stopped for a moment, waiting for Susan to ask a question. When she never did, Laura continued to tell her tale.

"Restricting population increase and then making a workforce that would not age and decreased production only seemed to make since to those in charge at the time." Laura stopped because the memories rushing back were making her choke up.

Susan finally spoke up, "What does this have to do with your father's death?"

"Nothing, nothing at all. Your eyes when I mentioned death, made me realize that you do not know why the world is like the way it is now. As for what my father said, he used to tell me, 'This Ranger's done fighting and flying.'" Laura spoke absently when she recounted the words of her father.

Looking confused, Susan asked, "What does that have anything to do with Edward, or Richard, or anything else going on?"

"Nothing, nothing at all." Laura spoke again, "and everything, in a way. I am tired of trying to figure it all out, and playing the games. I just want to continue with life and I am tired of fighting the battle."

"What battle?" Susan asked.

# FROM THE LOST TEXTS OF THE GRAND AUTHORS (AS ALWAYS THIS IS BELIEVED TO NOT BE THE ORIGINAL VERSION OF THE TEXT):

I'll tell you the truth: I don't care one way or the other. You only die once, and we all owe God a death. I won't do anything underhanded. If it's my fate, it's my fate. If not, not. No man is too good to serve his Ruler. Whatever happens, happens. If you die this year, you're paid up for next year. And it is known that cowards die many times before their deaths. The brave experience death only once. Of all the strange things I've ever heard, it seems most strange to me that men fear death, given that death, which can't be avoided, will come whenever it wants.

# LAURA

"Something my father told me, before he died." Laura started, realizing that Susan had no idea what she was talking about. "You know that I was one of the original five persons selected to be modified so many centuries ago." Laura paused. "As was Luke."

Laura started to think about how to tell Susan about what the time was like before the modification. How can she make it clear that we are in a better way than we were back then. Could she tell the full story of her father? Laura then wondered if she had ever told Luke about the last thing her father did.

"Wait, so you were around before all this came about?" Susan asked. Laura just looked sideways at her. Why did Susan think she looked so much younger and Luke looked so much older than everyone else?

"Yes, and it was a different time back then, people were much different. Society was getting out of control and five people were chosen to be part of an experiment. It was to see if the world could sustain itself with less people, if those people lived longer, and never passed their prime." Laura paused and continued, with "restricting population increase and then making a workforce that would not age and decreased production only seemed to make since to those in charge at the time." Laura began to choke up.

Susan finally spoke up, "What does this have to do with your father's death?"

"Nothing, nothing at all. Your eyes when I mentioned death, made me realize that you do not know why the world is like the way it is now. As for what my father said, he used to tell me, 'This Ranger's done fighting and flying.'" Laura spoke absently when she recounted the words of her father.

Laura's father was a boxer in the old time, but she remembered the stories that her mother used to tell her. His father was a drunk, a boxer, a former American Soldier, and an adulterer. She remembered this one time when they were going out somewhere when his mother and father were speaking.

"Daddy, are you coming?" Laura yells down the long yellow hallway of our house. Father had hate that color, but Mother had to have her way, or as her father would put it, "I won't get to have my way." Only years later did Laura know what he meant by that.

"Yeah, baby, I'm coming down." her father respond from his bathroom where everything was a labor of love for her parents. The shower took him more than three weeks to get just right; three shower heads, one in front, one in back, and a waterfall overhead. Father used to slide down the banister.

Mother would always say "You're going to scratch it or break your neck,"

Father would always respond "You put those in the wrong order. You should really be worried more about my neck. Neck ahead of furnishings,"

Looking confused, Alice asked, "What does that have anything to do with Edward, or Richard, or anything else going on?"

Broken out her trance to answer the question, "Nothing, nothing at all, and everything, in a way. I am tired of trying to figure it all out, and playing the games. I just want to continue with life and I am tired of fighting the battle." This was the total truth she was tired, but if she gave in like the other three, but if she did, what would happen to everything she helped build.

"What battle?" Susan asked.

"The battle we fight every day, how do we keep this society together? How do we keep our presence unknown? How much longer can this go on?"

"I don't find those to be a battle. I just think of them as part of life." Susan retorted.

"And that is what life has become for me. A battle, my mother wrote a story from my father's perspective of his last fight. After this is all over, would you like to read it?" Laura asked, hoping to change the subject.

The two got up and walked to the lift and began their descent to the lobby. All Laura could think about was her father saying, "This Ranger's done fighting and flying." So Laura sharing the lift just said, "This Elder is done fighting."

## FROM THE LOST TEXTS OF THE GRAND AUTHORS (AS ALWAYS THIS IS BELIEVED TO NOT BE THE ORIGINAL VERSION OF THE TEXT):

By my birth I rank above you, but don't be afraid of my greatness. Some are born great, some achieve greatness, and some have greatness thrust upon them. Your fate awaits you. Accept it in body and spirit. Go ahead. A happy new life is there if you want it. If you don't want it, just keep acting like a lowly servant who's not brave enough to grab the happiness there before him. Goodbye. Signed, Oxford.

# RICHARD

Waiting in the lobby of the Hall of the Future, Richard sat in one of the chairs waiting for the rest of the group, Richard started to prepare his next big action. Who would they leave behind? Thinking about himself in the looking glass before his descent, admiring his suit today. He was once again perfect looking, his tie has a perfect knot, but this time his tie had small diamonds that where a lighter black, his shoes were a matted black, there was not a hair out of place, and not a wrinkle in his black suit. Today he decided to go with a pearl-white shirt.

As everyone walked in, Richard was going to evaluate what they were wearing, and maybe that would help Richard decide who to spare.

The first was Alice, the trashiest of the Elder 13, who was still so low born, Richard felt shame for what he had done a few days ago. Not enough to not do it again, but still very bad. She as usual was wearing her normal short cut off shorts, along with a plaid button down shirt, which only had one button actually utilized for its purpose, the rest of the shirt was in one of two groups, the top part was separated so her tan breast would be visible as they were pushing the limit of the top of the shirt, while the bottom was tied in a knot allowing for her wonderful stomach to show.

Richard's thoughts drifted quickly to the knife that he pressed into her body in their dirty unauthorized sexual encounter, but he was just happy to know that she would be staying with him on this new society. Alice sat right down in the first chair which appeared from beneath. Alice did not smile at Richard, she merely just stared threw him as if he was a maggot. Richard knew this was odd because she had no right to look down on anyone.

The freak Kevin entered in his normal all black skimpy attire, with those hideous inkings covering every part of his skin not covered by his clothing. A small smile was under Richard's nose as he knew that Kevin would not be joining them on the other side of this reformation. His overly inked body would be put down like the cannibals from the historical times put forth by Mel Village countless years ago.

Next was the largest problem in the group, Laura, the second eldest Elder 13. Richard could see Kevin welcome the trashy child who decided to wear a pair of red yoga shorts with a white sweater with her usual symbol in the middle. For some reason, the side of this sweater had a silhouette of the hologram which features all the western retirements.

The second eldest was soon followed by the youngest Elder 13, Frederick who still had not updated his fashion. Richard believed he was too simple to pick a new style and stuck with just a reverse jumpsuit; however tonight, he was wearing a new color pattern: red with black accent colors on the edges. Richard was worried that the theme of red and black would drive him mad. So far Alice's shirt was red and black plaid, Kevin always wore black but he was showing a new inking of a red botonistic relic. Was Richard going to be the only one who maintained his own identity and just wear his black suit with his perfect pearl-white shirt.

Richard grew more impatient at the pattern of colored dress when Kimberly arrived, she did not wear her favorite red dress with black buttons, which much like Alice's buttons did not prescribe to their purpose. This dress however was long and black with lots of red buttons and a red shawl around her shoulders. Richard finally got a relief when Michael showed up in his normal long green floor length coat with brown buttons and blue shorts. His normal classical music shirt was replaced by a white shirt with a popular vegetable dish spelt incorrectly. There was no hint of red in his entire outfit. With this Richard had a good feeling for the outcome which was about to happen.

Richard noticed an odd look from Michael when Susan walked into the lobby and sat down right next to him. The look was not the normal look of wanting and lust, but of conquest and happiness. Susan's dress was a beautiful green sequin evening gown that was another sight for Richard's angry eyes. With the sea of a Laura inspired solidarity colors or red and black, the sight of green was a beautiful sight of two green beast which would soon be seen as allies.

Stephanie walked thru the lobby and sat down wearing something relatively new to Richard and the rest of the group looked in amaze at the vast transformation from her usual attire, as she was wearing all black with a black veil. She sat down and did not speak a word to anyone, then Richard remembered that Stephanie and Edward bonded over the pacification of Sector Two and Sector Five, they both thought Richard was being very extreme in his minor decision.

The group sat quietly waiting for almost a quarter of a standard unit waiting for the final two of the eleven invited Elder 13. Victoria finally showed her lowborn self in her un appealing dress, the only thought that Richard had to redeem this former food gather was that she did not wear anything red or black. Richard felt even more contempt for Victoria since his new evolution of Alice's stature.

Before the group could receive their final member, the front doors opened for the surprise that none of them expected. Grand Ruler, Michael Hollow, and the entire Grand Leadership walked thru the entrance of the Hall of the Future.

# FROM THE LOST TEXTS OF THE GRAND AUTHORS (AS ALWAYS THIS IS BELIEVED TO NOT BE THE ORIGINAL VERSION OF THE TEXT):

My George, sir, you're stubborn and suspicious. We come here to help you and you treat us like thugs, but you let a dirty more climb all over your daughter. Your whole family will be ruined. You ask who would dare speak this way and who is so cruel. I am one, sir, that comes to tell you your daughter and the more are now making the beast with two backs and preforming an unauthorized sexual encounter.

# KEVIN

Waiting in the lobby of the Hall of the Future, the front doors opened as Michael Hollow, and the entire Grand Leadership walked thru the entrance. No one spoke until one of the Grand Leaders spoke, as Kevin was sure that any attempt to take control of the situation would only validate the very thing they were trying to cover up. Michael Hollow spoke softly, "Who is in command here?"

Richard quickly responded, "No that you are here Grand Ruler, you are." As he left the front of the lobby and sat with the rest of the assembled Elder 13.

Kevin looked at the Grand Leadership, wondering why they would have come here. Michael Hollow quickly let them know, "I am sorry to hear about the man who leapt from the top of this building the other day, but I just wanted to let you know that we are doing everything we can, to insure that everything will go about just as it is supposed to be. We would not want anything to prevent our wonderful members of our society who for so long have given so much to not be rewarded with their retirement."

Richard stood up, Kevin was instantly worried. Richard walked over to the Grand Leadership and said, "Thank you all for coming here, I would just like to let you know that we are honored with your presence. Would you like a tour?"

Kevin quickly added, "Richard, I do not think the Grand Leadership would enjoy a tour, I am sure they have enough to do without spending their time looking at our arrangements. They are busy running the United European Kingdom."

This was met with universal agreed by all the Grand Leadership, but Richard's face started to turn red, "Well Kevin, I am sure that our guest would love to see something that they would not be allowed to see until their own two hundred and seventeenth name day. I ask you all to follow me."

Michael Hollow quickly looked interested, "Really you would let me see a view of Sector Seven?"

"But of course, you are the Grand Ruler, and as my associate put it, you run the entire United European Kingdom." Richard said, and then added with a bit of anger in his voice, "All by yourselves."

The group lead by Richard and Michael Hollow as the Grand Leadership and the Elder 13 followed behind them. Kevin could not hear what the two were saying so he simply followed the line of people deciding what to next ink his body with.

After several turns in the halls, Kevin did not recognize the door they were standing in front of. Richard spoke loudly, "Now Grand Ruler, and your Grand Leadership, please enter the room, where you will see everything you want to see when you reach your two hundred and seventeenth name day. Please enter." The Grand Ruler entered first, followed by the 7 members of the Grand Leadership, the Elder 13 started to file in, starting with Stephanie, then Frederick, Susan, Alice, Laura, Kimberly, Victoria, and finally himself. Richard followed behind Kevin and closed the door.

The Grand Ruler and the Grand Leadership all sat down in the chairs provided, while the Elder 13 who were present stood in front of them. Richard began speaking in a very dark voice. "Greetings 'Grand Ruler'" at his title he used sarcastic emphasis along with inverted commas with his hands, "This is the majority of the members of the Elder 13. NO! Do not bother speaking, all will be explained to your simple self. YOU are not in charge of anything. WE are. We are the reason that you think you are doing anything. The information you receive comes from us, the choices your 'Grand Leaders' give you come from us, but really there is only one correct answer. If you strive too far away from what is supposed to happen, you suddenly are no longer the Grand Ruler. We have been around for many successive generations, and you had no idea. However, now we are at a bit of a crossroad, WE do not exist, and our presence will undermine where we are currently holding the United European Kingdom together. No one wants us to end up like those broken provinces of 'Merica."

"Please, let me finish," Richard continued despite when Michael Hollow tried to speak. "I want this to go back to what used to happen, and what was the status quo. We need to be the main influences of the society, we need a puppet state to prop up and satisfy the various areas of the Kingdom. But this will no longer work. Our agreement, that granted you never knew about, will no longer work; but there is a solution." Richard smiled.

Kevin started thinking, when was the last time Richard smiled and something positive happened? Kevin was sure that today would not be that day.

"So I suppose we have two options: first we can prop up a new government, but of course that would take lots of time and energy; or second, we can just let you go back and work you like the puppet." After a long pause, Richard continued, "I suppose there is a third option: WE could take over, but then we would have to give up our life." At that Richard moved towards the door. "Alice, Laura, Michael, and Susan, come with me and we will let our fellow Elder 13 help the Grand Ruler and the Grand Leadership make up their mind.

At that command; Laura, Michael, and Susan walked towards the door, then after several moments Alice followed. Kevin thought it was odd that he would be left to help make up their mind, then he heard a click. Kevin spoke up, "Well gentlemen, what is your choice?"

The Grand Ruler spoke softly, "Well, I guess you have not left us with much of a decision."

At the word 'decision' Kevin remembered what that click sound was for, as thousands of liters of water started to filled the room. Kevin finally recognized the room they were in, they were in the scuba diving retirement room. Kevin resided himself into his certain death, as he sat down. The water flowed over his head and he was totally submerged. Kevin took in a deep breath, and felt the burning, the only positive from this burning is it would end soon.

And then, it did.

## FROM THE LOST TEXTS OF THE GRAND AUTHORS (AS ALWAYS THIS IS BELIEVED TO NOT BE THE ORIGINAL VERSION OF THE TEXT):

Oh, her grief has poisoned her mind. Oh, when bad things happen, they don't come one at a time, like enemy spies, but all at once like an army. The people are confused and spreading nasty rumors.

# LUKE

"Well, I guess you have not left us with much of a decision," the Grand Ruler spoke softly. Luke turned off the monitor for Sector Seven and shook his head.

"So I guess it comes to this?" Luke stood, and put on his vestments and walked to the lift, where he was stopped at his lift door by Richard, holding a rag in his hand which quickly was taken to Luke's face.

# FROM THE LOST TEXTS OF THE GRAND AUTHORS (AS ALWAYS THIS IS BELIEVED TO NOT BE THE ORIGINAL VERSION OF THE TEXT):

No! Come on, let's go to prison. The two of us together will sing like singers in a cage. We will be good to each other. We will think about the mysteries of the universe as if we were George's spies. In prison we'll outlast hordes of rulers that will come and go as their fortunes change. Anyone who wants to separate us will have to smoke us out of the cave of our togetherness like foxes. Wipe your eyes. Our jailers will shrivel up with old age before they make us cry again. We'll watch them starve to death first.

# LAURA

Sitting in their room, Laura and Luke stared at each other from each other's bed. Laura knew it was time. A fortnight had past, and it was time for the two to decide what to do. "Are we going to talk about this?" Laura asked.

Slowing raising his head from prayer, Luke started reciting, "I saw an angel come down from heaven, having the key of the bottomless pit and a great chain in his hand. And he laid hold on the dragon, that old serpent, which is the Devil, and Satan, and bound him a thousand years, and cast him into the bottomless pit, and shut him up, and set a seal upon him, that he should deceive the nations no more, till the thousand years should be fulfilled and after that he must be loosed a little season. And I saw thrones, and they sat upon them, and judgment was given unto them: and I saw the souls of them that were beheaded for the witness of Jesus, and for the word of God, and which had not worshipped the beast, neither his image, neither had received his mark upon their foreheads, or in their hands; and they lived and reigned with Christ a thousand years." Luke stopped for a moment, and then shook his head, "and whosoever was not found written in the book of life was cast into the lake of fire."

"As you have said, but that does not help our current situation, quote ancient text as much as you want, it does not get us out of this actual prison, this actual bottomless pit." Laura countered.

"What would you have me do?" Luke asked, already knowing the answer.

"Just do what Richard said, and we are free. We will rejoin the Elder 7. We will go back to our lives."

"I will not break my last vow, why can you not respect that?" Luke asked with tears in his eyes.

"Alice told us that it would only require a single time. It is something I not done many times. What are you scared of?" Laura asked, also already knowing the answer.

"The last time." With that, the conversation was over, and Luke started to return to his beads. Laura knew what he was referring to.

When they were first modified, the next day, as Luke explained it, the rapture came, and Jesus spoke to him personally, telling him, that he was a good person, but modifying his body in this way would be worse than any hell. He was going to receive the same punishment as the Morning Star, he was going to have to spend his life away.

"He will never come a third time. You are keeping your vows for nothing. Why torture yourself?" Laura asked, and silence answered.

# FROM SECTOR ONE GRAND WIRELESS SERVICE:

The Grand Ruler, Henry Ferguson, would just like to remind all people that his record high approval rating is because he listens to his Grand Leadership Council. The Sectors are doing better than ever, and there has not been a major issue for as long as this reporter has been journaling.

Henry Ferguson would like to convey this message from his Grand Leadership Council: Please do not be late for your appointment, whenever summoned. You have been waiting two hundred seventeen years for this day, don't waste any time getting what you truly deserve.

The United European Kingdom is at peace as it was, and always shall be.

# The Elder 13

# ABOUT THE AUTHOR

A school teacher in Texas, teaching English literature, Robert MacNeill has spent his life trying to figure out what he wanted to do with his life. He is still searching. After graduating High School, he joined the Army. After leaving the Army he worked in information technology, while going to school. Now he splits his time when he is not teaching with: coaching football, writing, narrating audiobooks, and occasionally sleeping.

His love of Shakespeare, should be evident by this point in the novel; but dystopian, fantasy, and science fiction is what tops his reading list.